THE GUNSMITH

465

The Children of Willow Springs

Books by J.R. Roberts
(Robert J. Randisi)

The Gunsmith series

Gunsmith Giant series

Lady Gunsmith series

Angel Eyes series

Tracker series

Mountain Jack Pike series

COMING SOON!

The Gunsmith
466 – Young Butch Cassidy

For more information visit:
www.SpeakingVolumes.us

THE GUNSMITH

465

The Children of Willow Springs

J.R. Roberts

SPEAKING VOLUMES, LLC
NAPLES, FLORIDA
2020

The Children of Willow Springs

ISBN 978-1-64540-360-9

Chapter One

Willow Springs, Nebraska

The Willow Springs Schoolhouse was on the outskirts of town. Bailey Wilkins walked there, stood back and watched as the children entered, filing past their teacher, some happily, some reluctantly. An attractive woman in her thirties, she wasn't what the man was there to see. He counted the children as they went inside, and then, after the teacher closed the door, he moved closer to inspect the building and its surroundings. The last thing he did was risk a look through one of the windows, and, as he did so, one child, a small girl, happened to look his way. She smiled, waved at him, and he found himself waving back.

Linda!" the teacher called out. "Stop staring out the window during the lesson."

"Yes, Mrs. Billig," the girl said.

The man ducked away, pleased that the girl hadn't given him up to the teacher. Quickly, he moved away from the school and started walking back to town.

***

Jane Billig had been teaching school for fifteen years but had only been in Willow Springs for three. She and her husband had come there from the East to start a new life, but within four months of arriving, he was suddenly dead. The doctor wasn't even sure what he had died of; it had happened in his sleep. But she had managed to survive being left alone, and much of her strength came from the kids she was teaching.

She saw the man watching from a distance, unsure if he was one of the fathers or not. But at that moment, he didn't seem to be a threatening presence. And when she caught Linda staring out the window, she didn't realize what the little girl was looking at.

Later, she wished she had been more concerned.

***

Bailey got back to town and, because it was too early for any of the saloons to be open, went to the Springhill Café, where he found Des Manning and Lyle Victor eating breakfast.

"There you are," Manning said. "I hope you got what I need."

"I got it," Bailey said.

"Then siddown, have some breakfast, and tell me."

Bailey sat and waved frantically at a waiter, who came over and took his order of ham-and-eggs.

"Here," Manning said, pouring him a cup of coffee. "Now come on, tell me."

"The school ain't near any other buildings," Bailey started. "There's fifteen kids in the class—at least, that's how many was there this mornin'. The teacher is a pretty woman."

"Did she see you?"

"No."

"Are you sure?"

Bailey took a sip of coffee before saying, "Yup."

Manning leaned forward. Victor was eating as if he was afraid someone was going to take his plate. That was probably because he had spent half his life in prison. So he just kept eating and listening.

"Did anybody see you?" Manning asked.

"Well . . . one little girl," Bailey said.

"How'd that happen?"

"I looked in the window, and she happened to look out at the same time. No big deal."

"What did she do?"

"She waved at me."

"And what did you do?"

"What could I do?" Bailey said. "I waved back."

Manning laughed. The waiter came over and put Bailey's plate in front of him.

"You see any other adults near the schoolhouse?" Manning asked.

"No," Bailey said, "the kids all seemed to get to school by themselves."

"That's good," Manning said.

Around a mouthful of eggs Bailey said, "I don't understand, I thought we was here to look at the bank, not a schoolhouse."

"Never mind," Manning said. "Just let me do the thinkin' and everythin' will go fine." Manning looked at Lyle Victor. "Right, Lyle?"

"Whatever you say, boss," Victor replied.

"See?" Manning said to Bailey.

"I get it, boss," Bailey said, "I get it."

"So just pay attention to your breakfast," Manning said and turned his attention back to his own plate.

Chapter Two

Willow Springs was a quiet town. Sheriff Ed Crown had little to do but toss a drunk or two in a cell every so often. A lawman for forty years, he had taken the job because it was an easy one.

When Clint Adams rode into town, Crown was happy to see him. They had been friends for many years, had ridden together on many adventures. He had invited Clint to town years ago, but this was the first time Clint had come.

On Clint's third day in town, they were sitting in the Willow Springs Café, having breakfast.

"You seem to really have it made here, Ed," Clint said. "This really does seem like a nice, quiet town."

"It is," Crown said. "It's a great place for me to finish out my career as a lawman."

"Well," Clint said, "I have to admit I'm more used to seeing you active. I've seen you chase outlaws to hell and back, with or without a posse."

"Those were the old days, Clint," Crown said. "You're lookin' at a shell of the man I once was. Besides, more than once I had you to back me up."

Crown had grey hair and a heavily lined face, but he stood tall and was still in good shape, as far as Clint could see.

"You look to me like you still got a few more years in you, Ed."

"Well," Crown said, "I've got a wife now. I didn't have a woman back in my hellion days. Margaret wants me to retire and settle down."

They both finished their breakfasts and pushed their plates away, then had a final cup of coffee.

"By the way, Margaret wants to know when you're finally gonna come to supper? You've been here a couple of days, already."

"Clint had meant to accept the invitation the first day it was given, but he had met a woman named Florence, and they spent that first night together. And the second. But Florence had left town on the morning stage.

"I'll come tonight, if that's okay," Clint said.

"That'd be great," Crown said. "I'll tell Maggie. She'll be thrilled. She's been wantin' to meet you."

"I want to meet her, too," Clint said.

Crown finished his coffee and grabbed his hat.

"I've got some business," he said. "You know where the house is. We'll see you there at six."

"I'll be there," Clint promised.

Sheriff Ed Crown turned and left the café. Clint called the waiter over.

"What do I owe you?" he asked.

"You ate with the sheriff, sir," the waiter said. "There's no charge."

Clint had known many lawmen to accept food and drink for free, but never Ed Crown. Apparently, age had changed him in more ways than one.

***

Down the street at the Springhill Café, three men were also finishing their breakfast.

"So what's next boss?" Bailey asked Manning.

"I ain't decided how to play it, yet," Manning admitted. "I think I might have to go and talk to my wife, first."

"Your wife?" Bailey asked.

"Well, my ex-wife," Manning said. "My daughter's mother. I'm gonna give her a chance to change her mind."

"About what?" Bailey asked.

"That's not important now," Manning said. "You boys look after yourselves and don't get into trouble." He stood up. "I'll see you later at the Summerhill Saloon."

As he stood up and left, Lyle Victor said, "I need more coffee."

Bailey stood up, said, "Pay the bill after you're done," and left.

***

Manning stopped just outside the house he had once shared with his wife, Diane. But she had kicked him out and divorced him four years ago, when their daughter was only two years old. Since then, Manning had been trying to be a part of his daughter's life, and Diane kept fighting him. Today he was giving her one last chance to change her mind.

He went up the walk and knocked on the front door. When it opened and Diane Manning saw him, her eyes widened.

"No," she said, "oh, no," and tried to close the door, but he put his hand out and stopped it.

"We have to talk," he said.

"Des," she said, "I have nothin' to say to you."

"Well," he replied, pushing his way into the house, "I have some things to say to you."

Chapter Three

Diane Manning glared at her ex-husband, glad that her daughter was in school.

"If I had my gun, I'd kill you, right now," she said to him, looking over at her rifle hanging on the wall.

"Jesus, Diane," Manning said. "Was I that bad?"

"Worse!" she spat.

"Look, I just wanna see my daughter."

"Not a chance," she said. "I don't want you near her."

Manning studied his ex-wife. He wondered how a woman so beautiful could be so mean? He looked around at the meager furnishings in the small house.

"Do you like livin' like this?" he asked.

"You think I'd be better off livin' with you?" she asked. "I'm lucky you didn't kill me."

"I know, I know," he said, "I hit you a coupla times—"

"You nearly beat me to death, Des," she said. "And for no good reason. You were just drunk."

"I don't get that way no more, Diane," Manning said. "I swear."

"Swear it to somebody else," she said. "I don't wanna hear it."

"You bitch—" Manning started, taking a step toward her.

"Go ahead," she said, "beat me again, see where that gets you."

"I ain't gonna beat ya," he growled at her. "I'm gonna do worse."

He turned and stormed out of the house.

She went to the window to watch him walk away, just to be sure he was gone. Then she wondered what could be worse than a beating?

***

At three o'clock Jane Billig sent all the children home from school. She stood in the doorway and watched them all leave. The last one was little Linda Manning, who just sort of skulked out of the schoolhouse with her head down.

"Linda, are you all right?" she asked.

"No, Ma'am,"

Jane crouched down in front of the girl.

"What's wrong?"

"How come everybody else in school's got a momma and a poppa, and I don't?" she asked.

"Linda, I believe you have a poppa."

"Yeah, but he ain't been around," Linda said. "Why is that?"

"I don't know, sweetie," Jane said. "Have you asked your mother?"

"Yes, Ma'am," Linda said, "but she don't talk about him."

"I think you'll just have to keep asking her, Linda," Jane said, "until she decides to give you an answer."

"Yes, Ma'am."

"Now you run along home," Jane said. "I see some of the older children are waiting for you."

"Yes, Ma'am."

Jane stood and watched as Linda ran to an older girl and boy who were neighbors of hers and would walk her home. She watched as the three of them walked away, then looked around to see if there was any sign of the man she had seen earlier. Satisfied that no one was there, she turned and went back into the schoolhouse.

***

Sheriff Ed Crown went home to tell his wife, Margaret, that they had a guest for supper that night.

"It's about time," she said. "I been waitin' to meet this friend of yours."

"Well, you're gonna meet 'im," Crown said, "and I want you to show him how you make the best fried chicken he ever ate."

"I'll do that, Ed Crown, if you promise me one thing."

"What's that?"

"Before you come home tonight, you'll go over to the Bayliss Barbershop and take a bath."

"Aw, Maggie—"

"You heard me, you old coot," Margaret said, "no bath, no chicken."

"I reckon that's somethin' I can't say no to," Crown admitted.

He tried to hug his wife, but she backed away from him and said, "Not til after your bath."

"Not only will I take a bath," he promised her, "but I'll use some of that bay rum Bayliss has got."

"Not too much of it," she said. "I want you to smell clean, not sickly sweet."

"Tarnation," he said, "if you ain't the most demandin' woman."

"Fried chicken, Ed Crown," she said.

"Awright, awright," he said, "I'll keep my side of the bargain."

"Then git," she said, "I don't want to see you back here until suppertime—and you better be clean!"

Chapter Four

Clint stopped in the Summerhill Saloon for one beer before going to supper at Sheriff Ed Crown's house. While he was standing at the bar, a man came bursting through the batwing doors and joined two more men at a table. He was very angry about something.

"Get me a beer!" he snapped at one of the other men.

One of the men came to the bar and said to the bartender, "A beer."

"Your friend seems real upset," the barman said, setting the beer down on the bar.

"Wives will do that to ya," the man said, and carried the beer back to the table.

"I'm glad I ain't married," the bartender said to Clint. "You?"

"Nope," Clint said, "never got around to it. I don't think I ever will."

The bartender was about Clint's age, said, "Fellas our age are pretty set in our ways."

"I think you're right," Clint said.

Lyle Victor put the beer down in front of Manning, who grabbed it and drank half of it.

"I guess it didn't go so well?" Bailey asked.

"She's just as much a bitch as ever," Manning said. "I should've given her a good beatin'."

"That's what some women need to keep 'em in line," Victor said.

Manning glared at the man.

"Nobody asked you for your opinion, Victor," he said. "Just drink your beer."

Lyle Victor did as he was told.

"So," Bailey asked Manning, "are we ready to take the bank?"

"Almost," Manning said. "I just have a few more details to clear up first."

"Like what?"

"I'll let you know when it's done," Manning said. "Until then, you and Victor stay out of trouble. You got it?"

"No," Bailey said, "but I'll do my best."

Manning looked up at the bar where one man was talking to the bartender.

"Lyle, who's that at the bar?" he asked.

"Beats me," Victor said. "He wasn't talkin' when I went up to get your beer."

At that moment the man left the bar and walked out of the saloon.

"Whataya care who some stranger is?" Bailey asked.

"I don't," Manning said. "And it don't matter because he's gone." He went back to his beer.

***

When the front door of her house opened, Margaret Crown hurried from the kitchen to see her husband entering the house. She could see that he had not only had a bath, but a haircut and a shave, as well.

"Well," she said, "what an improvement."

"I thought you'd be happy."

He went to his wife and enveloped her in a huge hug.

"And I see you didn't go for the bay rum," she said, hugging him back.

"And is that your friend chicken I smell?" he asked.

"It certainly is," she said, "and my parsley potatoes."

"I wanted to give my friend a good supper," he said, "but after eatin' this meal, he ain't gonna wanna leave."

"He'll have to," she said. "I'm not about to share you with anyone. Now help me set the table."

***

Clint followed Ed Crown's directions and walked to the sheriff's house. When he knocked on the door, it was opened by Crown.

"Right on time!" Crown said, shaking Clint's hand and drawing him into the house. "Come on, I want ya to meet the Mrs."

Clint followed Crown into a sparsely furnished living room. Off to one side was a table that was set with three places for supper.

"Maggie, get out here and meet our guest!" Crown shouted.

When Margaret Crown came out of the kitchen, Clint was surprised. Ed Crown was in his mid-sixties, but his wife looked to be in her early forties and was a lovely woman.

"Maggie, this is Clint Adams," Crown said. "Clint, my wife, Maggie."

"It's a pleasure to finally meet you," she said. "Ed's always talkin' about you."

"Well, he never stops talking about his beautiful wife," Clint said, taking her hand, "and I can see why."

"I told you he was a charmer," Crown said, as his wife blushed. "I can see I ain't gonna be able to leave you two alone."

"Get Clint a drink, Ed," she said, "and I'll go back to the kitchen and get supper on the table."

"It smells wonderful," Clint told her.

"Never mind how it smells," Crown said. "Wait til you taste it."

"That's what I've been waiting for," Clint admitted.

Chapter Five

As promised, Margaret Crown's fried chicken was the best Clint had ever tasted. She was very pleased with his compliments and kept bringing out more pieces until he begged off.

"I'm stuffed, Margaret," he said, rubbing his stomach. "I couldn't eat another bite."

"I hope that's not true," she said. "I made a peach cobbler for dessert."

"In that case," he said, "I'll force myself to have some."

"You and Ed relax and digest a bit, and I'll bring out the cobbler and coffee shortly."

Crown and Clint got up from the table and went to sit on the sofa.

"How about a whiskey?" Crown asked. "Or are you still strictly a beer man?"

"I am," Clint said, "but I'll take a small one."

"Good!" Crown rushed across the room to pour two shot glasses and returned to the sofa.

"Get that down before Maggie comes out," Crown instructed.

"She doesn't like drinking?" Clint asked.

"Not at all," Crown said, tossing his down. Clint drank his, and Crown took the two empty glasses back across the room.

Moments later, Margaret came out of the kitchen with the cobbler and coffee.

"Come and get it, gents," she said. "And I hope you didn't fill up on whiskey."

"We just had a drop each," Crown assured her.

They went to the table and waited while she dished out the cobbler and passed them each a plate.

"This is amazing," Clint said, after the first bite. "You're a lucky man, Ed."

"I know it," Crown said.

"And when will you be getting married, Clint?"

Clint choked on his sip of coffee and said, "I don't think that's in the cards for me, Margaret."

"Just call me Maggie," she said, "and maybe while you're here, we can introduce you to someone. I have several friends who would make any man a fine wife."

"I'm sure they would," Clint said, "but I don't know how much longer I'll be in town."

"Well," Margaret said, "why don't we see what we can do while you *are* here?"

Clint looked at Ed Crown, who shrugged helplessly.

***

Completely full, from Margaret's chicken and cobbler, Clint made his way back to his hotel. It was the oldest hotel in town, which meant there were no gas lamps. He had to light a lamp as he entered his room, just as the chandelier lamps had to be lighted in the lobby.

In his room, he immediately removed his gunbelt and the belt from his trousers. Finally, he was able to breathe more freely. But as full as he was, he was also very satisfied with the meal. And his friend seemed to be very happy with his much younger wife.

He had no specific plans as to how long he would stay in Willow Springs, but Maggie Crown seemed intent on matching Clint with a wife, which was a good enough reason for him to leave town—especially since Florence had already left.

Perhaps, after breakfast, he would make his final decision.

***

"Are you sure you want to play it that way?" Bailey asked Manning.

It was late, and they were sitting at a table in the Summerhill Saloon.

"Most bank jobs fail because of poor plannin'," Manning said. "This one I've planned perfect."

"Yeah, but—"

"Believe me," Manning said, "you just have to give people somethin' else to worry about."

"Yeah, but this—"

"Bailey," Manning said, "if you don't wanna be part of this, then you can walk away."

"No, no," Bailey said, "I ain't sayin' that." He looked at Lyle Victor. "Whatayou think, Lyle?"

Manning spoke before Victor could answer.

"It don't matter what he thinks," he said. "He's in. The question is, are you?"

"I'm in, Des," Bailey said. "Yeah, I'm in."

"We're each gonna have a job to do," Manning said. "If we do them, this will go off without a hitch. Do you understand me?"

"Got it, boss," Victor said.

"I guess I'll understand better when you explain the whole thing to us," Bailey said.

Manning looked around, making sure there was no one else within earshot. Other tables were occupied, so he lowered his voice.

"Here's what we're gonna do . . ."

Chapter Six

When Clint woke the next morning, he immediately smelled smoke.

"What the hell—" he said, getting out of bed and quickly pulling on his trousers and strapping on his gun. He ran out into the hall and saw the smoke. First, he ran to the stairs, but it was plain that the fire was raging in the lobby. Smoke was coming up the stairs, and there was no way out that way.

He started running up and down the hall, banging on doors and yelling, "Fire, fire!" to wake other guests. As it turned out, many of them were already awake and out of their rooms. By the time he got the rest out into the hall, there seemed to be a dozen, maybe a few more, including women and some small children.

"Oh my God," one woman yelled. "We're gonna die."

"We're not going to die," Clint called out. "We just need to find another way down. We're cut off from the lobby."

"What about a back way?" one man asked.

"There's no back stairway."

"The gas will explode," another man said, causing two of the women to scream.

"This is an old hotel," Clint said. "There are no gas lines, so there's no danger of an explosion. We just have to get out before the fire gets up here."

Everyone was now coughing and covering their mouths, and the children were crying.

"What about the roof?" a male guest asked.

"We'd be trapped up there," Clint said.

He remembered that there were rooms on both sides of the hotel. Some of the windows overlooked an alley, and the other side an empty lot.

"Let's get to the other side of the hotel," he said. "Hurry. Follow me."

"Why should we follow you?" one man asked.

"Because I have an idea," Clint said. "If you don't want to follow me, then stay here and die."

Clint led the way, and the guests began to follow.

***

Ed Crown looked up from his desk as the door to his office slammed open.

"Sheriff!" a man shouted. "The hotel's on fire!"

"Which one?" Crown asked, coming out of his seat.

"The Winterhill."

"That old place is a tinderbox," Crown said. "It'll go up in no time. What about our fire department?"

"The volunteers are on the way."

Crown ran from his office with the man following him. From down the street he could see flames shooting out of the first floor of the hotel, and smoke coming from the second floor windows. He knew Clint was in that hotel.

From behind him, he heard the fire bell and saw the volunteer fire fighters hurrying to the fire. He turned to the man who had run into his office.

"Otis, get more men!"

"Yes, sir."

Crown reached the hotel at the same time as the fire fighters.

"We need a bucket brigade!" he shouted.

"Jesus," one of the firefighters said, "this place is so old—"

"Never mind!" Crown shouted. "Just get to it."

A crowd had gathered, and now a man broke from it and approached Crown.

"Sheriff, somethin's happenin' on the other side of the hotel."

Crown ran around to the empty lot that ran alongside the hotel. On the second floor, he saw a window open and a man's head came out.

It was Clint Adams.

***

"Okay," Clint said, turning from the window to look at the people who had crowded into the room. Behind them the hallway filled with smoke. "This is what we're going to do. Get the sheet off that bed."

Two men stripped the bed and grabbed the sheet.

"I need four men to jump out this window."

"What? We'll break our necks," one man said.

"We'll hold one end of the sheet and lower you down as far as we can. Then you let go. It won't be a long drop."

"The children can't do that!" a woman complained.

"I know," Clint said. "Once there are four men on the ground, we'll toss the sheet down. Then you each grab a corner. You're going to catch the rest of us as we jump out—especially the women and children. Got it?"

"We got it," a man said, then looked at the others. "Come on."

There were six men, so Clint and one man were going to have to lower the others down.

"Let's get started," Clint said.

Chapter Seven

As the first man stuck his legs out the window and sat on the windowsill, Clint said, "Remember, bend your knees when you hit and roll."

They lowered him as far as they could, but he still had about eight feet to drop. He let go, hit the ground and rolled, came up waving.

"I'm good. Next!"

They did this three more times, and by the time the four men were on the ground, a small crowd had gathered to see what was going on.

Clint dropped the sheet down and yelled, "Grab all four corners and spread it. We'll drop the children first, then the women."

The four men caught the sheet and spread it. As Clint leaned out the window with each child and dropped them, the four men caught them in the sheet.

One small boy exclaimed, "Can we do that again!" as he was hustled away by women in the crowd.

Clint turned to the remaining people in the room, three women and a man.

"Ladies next," he said.

"Are you sure they'll catch us?" the youngest one, in her twenties, asked.

"Oh, they'll catch you, don't worry. Come on, we don't have much time. This whole place is going to go up in minutes."

He helped her up onto the windowsill, grabbed her hands and lowered her as far as he could, then dropped her. She screamed but landed right in the center of the tautly spread sheet.

"Come on!" he said to the next one.

He lowered her, did the same, and she was caught. The last woman was in her sixties.

"I think this is gonna break my bones," she said.

"Better than burnin' to death," the other man said.

"I guess."

Clint lowered her and dropped her. She landed without breaking a nail.

"Okay, friend," Clint said. "Your turn."

"I'm goin'," he said.

He leaped up onto the windowsill and just dropped, landing heavily in the sheet so that his butt almost struck the ground. But he was safe.

Clint was about to jump out when he heard a woman screaming.

"Help! Help! My baby!"

He turned.

***

Sheriff Crown got to the empty lot as Clint was dropping the last woman.

"Everybody okay?" he asked.

"He saved us," the youngest woman said, pointing up at Clint.

Crown looked up, saw Clint leaning out the window, but quickly withdraw. Then he saw a man jump out and land in the sheet. Again, he saw Clint lean out and stop.

"Clint, come on!" he yelled. "You don't have long."

"There's a woman up here with a baby somewhere," Clint shouted. "I've got to find them."

"Clint!" Crown shouted as he withdrew. "Don't be crazy."

"He's gonna burn," somebody said.

***

Clint turned and went to the door. The smoke in the hall was thick.

"Hello?" he called. "Where are you?"

"Back here," a woman called. "Oh, help me! Help my baby!"

Clint got out into the hall and followed the sound of the voice to the back of the hotel.

"In here!" she shouted.

He tried the door of the first room in the hall, found it locked.

"Stand back from the door," he called.

"I—I can't get out of bed!" she called back.

He drove his shoulder into the door, snapping it open. Inside he found a woman on the bed, holding a small infant. She was either ill, or had just given birth, it really didn't matter.

"Oh, thank God!" she said. "Please, get us out of here."

"There's only one way out," he told her, "and that's the window."

He picked up a chair and tossed it through the window, sure the sound would catch everyone's attention on the ground. When he looked out, he saw the four men with the sheet moving toward him.

"I've got a woman and a baby up here. Get ready to catch them!"

"We got 'er!" one of the men called.

Clint turned to the young woman on the bed.

"Okay, let's go," he said.

"I can't," she said. "My baby—"

"You're going first," Clint said. "Let me have the baby."

He helped her out of bed, then took the baby and laid it back on the bed.

"What are you doing?" she asked, panicky.

"I have to lower you down," he said. "They're going to catch you in a sheet."

"But the baby—"

"I'll be right behind you with the baby."

"Y-you ain't gonna drop her out the window, are ya?" she asked.

"No," he said, "I'll be holding her when I jump. Now come on!"

He grabbed her and yanked her to the window, then pushed her out, lowered her down and dropped her. She landed right in the center of the sheet.

"Okay, little one," he said, as smoke filled the room, "it's you and me."

He grabbed the baby, moved to the window, dangled his legs and then dropped out, holding the baby close to his chest. If he had fallen feet first, it might have been a problem, but he fell in a prone position, landing on his back in the sheet. When the men put him on his feet, the woman came running over to him. The people gathered around and started to applaud.

"Oh, thank you, thank you!" she cried, taking the baby from him.

While Clint was coughing, trying to get his breathe, Ed Crown came over and said, "You're crazy!"

Chapter Eight

Earlier that morning it was Bailey Wilkins who had entered the lobby of the hotel. His instructions were clear: start a fire. He looked around, and the easiest way he could see to do that was the chandelier. He was holding a shotgun, so he simply raised the barrel and fired. The chandelier shattered, and the flames from each lamp came down, fanning out. Immediately, the wood of the furniture, and the floor, caught fire, and the flames spread.

Bailey backed out and ran down the street toward the bank, where Manning and Victor were waiting.

"It's done!" he told Manning.

"All right," Manning said, looking across at the bank. "Let's wait for everyone's attention to be on the hotel, and then we'll go in."

Eventually, they heard the bell of the fire brigade, and people running toward the hotel. Finally, some customers and employees came out of the bank to see what was happening.

"Okay," Manning said, "let's do it. Lyle, stay outside with the horses and watch for the law."

"Right, boss."

They walked across the street with their horses, then handed the reins to Victor, who mounted his own and looked off down the street toward the fire.

"Keep a sharp eye all around you!" Manning snapped. "Not just down the street."

"Right."

Manning drew his gun, and Bailey took his shotgun into the bank.

A couple of employees were standing by the widow glancing over at them.

"Just stand easy," Manning said, "and nobody'll get hurt."

"Oh," a middle-aged woman said.

"Who's the teller?" Manning asked.

"I am," a small man said.

"And where's the manager?"

"In his office," the woman said.

"Get 'im!"

The woman walked across the floor, with Manning following her.

Bailey pointed his shotgun at the teller and said, "Get behind your cage."

The teller raised his hands and walked to his cage.

The woman knocked on the manager's door, and the man came out, wearing a three-piece suit.

"What is it, Mrs. King—wha—"

Manning stuck his gun in the man's face.

"You're opening the safe," he said. "Right now!"

***

While the fire brigade worked to keep the flames from spreading to nearby buildings, people Clint had helped to rescue were cared for by others. A doctor moved in-and-out among them, stopping near Clint.

"I'm okay, Doc," Clint said, wiping his face and eyes with a wet cloth somebody had given him. "Look after the kids—and that baby."

"The baby's fine," the doctor said. "So's the mother, thanks to you."

Ed Crown was standing nearby.

"All those people you dropped out the window are fine," he said. "That was a great idea. You saved every last one, Clint."

"I'd like to know how that fire started," Clint said, as the doctor moved away.

"Well, now that I know you're okay," Crown said, "I'll see if I can find the desk clerk."

"I'll come with you," Clint said, standing and setting the cloth aside.

Chapter Nine

Crown and Clint found the desk clerk, still standing outside the burning hotel, watching. The fire brigade had managed to soak the building on the other side of the hotel, keeping the rest of the street from going up.

"Billy," Crown said, to the clerk, "do you know what started the fire?"

"I sure do, Sheriff," the young man said. "A fella came in with a shotgun and shot the chandelier down."

"Deliberately?" Crown asked.

"It sure looked like it."

Crown looked at Clint.

"Why would somebody do that?" he said.

"To kill people in the hotel," Clint suggested, "or as a distraction."

"Distraction?"

"Sure," Clint said. "He wanted everybody to be looking at the burning hotel."

"But why?"

"So they wouldn't be looking at something else."

Suddenly, they heard shots.

"Damn it!" Crown said.

"Sheriff, sheriff," somebody shouted. "They're robbin' the bank."

"The bank!" Crown said.

He and Clint started running.

***

"Come on, come on," Manning snapped at the slow moving bank manager, who was filling bags from the safe.

"I-I'm going as fast as I can—I can't . . . breathe very well—"

"Yeah, yeah," Manning said, "have a heart attack after you fill those bags!" He turned his head and shouted to Bailey. "You got the money from out there?"

"All set," Bailey said.

"Check outside."

Bailey went to the door and looked out the window. Lyle Victor signaled to him that everything was okay.

"So far, so good," Bailey called back to Manning.

"Oh God," the bank manager said. He clutched his chest and slid down onto his face.

"Shit!" Manning snapped. He reached down and picked up the two money bags. He could see there was more money in the safe, but didn't feel they had the time, so the two bags—and what they got from the teller's cages—would have to do.

Then, as he was starting to turn, he saw the bank manager's hand reaching into the safe. That's when he knew there was a gun there.

"Don't—" he warned, then he decided just to shoot and be done with it. He fired twice, and the manager jerked, then stiffened.

Bailey, hearing the shots, panicked and pulled the trigger on his shotgun. The blast knocked the teller off his feet and shredded him.

"Oh, God!" the female employee cried out.

Bailey turned to her and pulled the trigger again, but both barrels had been discharged.

"Let's go!" Manning yelled, heading for the door. "Those shots are gonna be heard."

Manning and Bailey rushed out to where Victor was holding the horses. A man standing across the street decided to try to be a hero and went for his gun. Manning shot him dead, then mounted his horse.

"Let's get outta here!" he shouted.

The three bank robbers turned their horses and began to ride up the street.

***

Crown and Clint heard the shotgun blasts as they ran toward the bank, then heard a shot on the street. As they came within sight of the bank, they saw the three men riding away. Ed Crown fired several shots, but they were out of range.

"Check on him," he said to Clint, pointing across the street.

Clint ran to the citizen who was down and saw there was no use. He was dead. As he stood up, he saw Crown coming out of the bank.

"They killed the teller and the manager and emptied the safe," Crown said. "Damn it, this is what the fire was all about."

"What do you want to do, Ed?"

"Go after them!"

"Then I'm with you."

"Let's grab those horses," Crown said, pointing.

There were several horses tied off in front of a saloon. Crown and Clint ran to them and grabbed two. As they mounted up, some men came out of the saloon.

"Hey," one of them shouted, "those are our horses."

"You'll get 'em back!" Crown called back.

He and Clint started riding after the bank robbers.

***

As they got outside of town, Manning suddenly stopped and looked back. At that moment no one was chasing them.

Bailey and Victor reined in beside him.

"What are ya doin'?" Bailey asked. "We gotta go."

"Yeah, we do," Manning said, "but this way."

"Where—"

"We're goin' to the schoolhouse," Manning said and urged his horses into a run.

"The schoolhouse?" Bailey said, looking at Victor.

Lyle Victor shrugged and lit out after Manning.

Chapter Ten

Crown and Clint got outside of town and reined in their horses.

"What is it?" Crown asked.

"They stopped here, then lit out that way," Clint said, pointing.

"Why would they do that?" Crown asked. "You'd think they'd be ridin' outta town."

"What's that way?" Clint asked.

"The schoolhouse."

"Why would they be going to the schoolhouse?" Clint asked.

"I don't know," Crown said, "but I don't like it. We'd better go see."

They turned their horses and rode toward the schoolhouse.

***

Manning reined in his horse in front of the schoolhouse. Bailey and Victor came along behind him as he dismounted.

"Wait out here," he told them, and went inside.

Jane Billig was startled and straightened her spine as Manning entered.

"What are you doing?" she asked. "Are you a parent?"

"That's right," he said. "I'm here for my girl."

"Who's your child?" Mrs. Billig asked.

"Linda Manning," he said.

"Pa?"

He turned his head, looked at the six-year-old girl who had stood up. "Pa, is that you?"

"It's me, honey," he said. "I've come to take you with me."

"Oh, Pa—"

"Linda," Mrs. Billig said sternly, "sit back down."

The little girl sat.

"I can't let you take her until I hear from her mother," Mrs. Billig said. "I don't know you, sir."

"She knows me, don't ya, honey?"

The little girl stared at him but didn't say anything.

"Linda?" Manning said.

"I'll have to ask you to leave, sir," Mrs. Billig said.

That was when he heard horses outside.

***

Outside the schoolhouse Bailey said to Lyle Victor, "What the hell are we doin' here?"

Victor just shrugged.

At that moment, they heard horses coming.

"We better get inside," Bailey said.

They both dismounted and ran to the schoolhouse door. Bailey looked back, saw two riders, recognized one as the sheriff, then followed Victor inside. Bailey was carrying the bags of money from the bank.

***

Both Mrs. Billig and Manning turned to look at the door as it opened, and the two men darted in.

"I told you to wait outside," Manning said.

"It's the sheriff and another man," Bailey said. "We should've headed out of town. Whatawe do now?"

Manning thought a moment, then looked around.

"We got a schoolhouse full of kids," he said. "They ain't gonna come in here."

"You can't do that," the teacher said. "You can't endanger these children. You have to leave."

"You shuddup and sit down, lady," Manning ordered.

"I'll do no such thing—"

Manning pulled his gun and pointed it at her.

"You'll do as you're told."

"Pa!" Linda cried out.

"Keep quiet, girl," Manning said.

"That's your daughter?" Bailey asked.

"That's her," Manning said, moving to the window. He saw the two riders approaching. "It's the sheriff, all right, and he's got that fella from the saloon. We never did find out who he is."

"It don't matter," Bailey said. "There's only two of 'em. We gotta take care of 'em before more come."

Manning looked around, didn't see a back door.

"We can get out of here without shootin'," he said. "We just gotta play it right."

"And how's that?" Bailey asked.

"Just gimme a minute," Manning said.

***

"They're inside," Sheriff Crown said. "They got the kids as hostages. What the hell do we do now?"

"We'll have to talk them out," Clint said.

They both dismounted. The sheriff walked over to the robbers' three horses.

"There's no money here," he said. "They got it inside with them."

"I'm not worried about the money," Clint said. "It's the kids."

43

"I know," Crown said, "and the teacher, Jane Billig."

"It's up to you, Sheriff," Clint said. "What do you want to do?"

Chapter Eleven

"Cover those windows," Manning told Bailey and Victor. Bailey put the money bags down at his feet.

The two men moved to the front windows.

"What are you planning to do?" Mrs. Billig asked. She was sitting at her desk, looking worried.

"Well," Manning said, "I guess I'm gonna start by talkin' to the sheriff."

"Let the children go—"

"And you're gonna start by shuttin' up," he snapped, cutting her off.

He walked to the door and opened it a crack.

"Sheriff, can you hear me?"

"I hear you," the sheriff called back.

"We got fifteen kids in here," Manning yelled. "If you charge this building, we'll start shootin' 'em."

"What do you want?" the sheriff called.

"You just stay where you are," Manning replied, "and I'll let you know." He closed the door, turned and looked at the teacher.

"You got anythin' to drink in here?" he asked.

***

"What do you think they're gonna ask for?" Crown asked Clint.

"Safe passage out of town," Clint said. "And they might take the teacher and some kids with them."

"That's just what we need," Crown said. "I can't let them take those kids, Clint."

"That's what I was thinking."

Crown looked around, didn't see anyone else in the area.

"At least nobody else is here," he said.

"I'd still like to know why, when they already had the bank money, they decided to come to the schoolhouse," Clint said. "There must be something in there they want."

"Or somebody," Crown said.

"You think one of these bank robbers has a child in this school?"

"Could be."

"Still . . . they have to know they're going to be ducking a posse for some time. Why would they want to have a kid along?"

"Maybe one of them is a father who just wanted to say goodbye," Crown suggested.

"Well, whatever the reason, they're in there now," Clint said, "and we've got to get them out."

"How do you suggest we do that?" Crown asked.

"We'll have to start by talking to them," Clint said, "and bargaining."

"What have we got to bargain with?"

"That's what we've got to figure out."

***

"I have nothing to drink in here," Mrs. Billig said. "This is a school, not a saloon."

"She's got a mouth on her," Bailey said, from the window. "How are we gonna get out of here, Des?"

"We got the advantage, Bailey," Manning said.

"We do?"

Manning nodded.

"We got this teacher, and these kids," he said. "We're gonna use them to keep us safe."

"Why don't we shoot a kid and toss it out the door?" Lyle Victor suggested. "That'll show 'em we mean business."

The three adults in the building stared at him for a few moments.

"You wouldn't do that," Mrs. Billig said. "You couldn't."

Bailey looked at Manning.

"I told you a long time ago, he's quiet, but he's the crazy one."

"Lyle, just keep your mouth shut and keep lookin' out that window," Manning said. "I don't need any suggestions from you."

Victor shrugged and stared out the window.

"Just an idea," he said.

Manning looked at Mrs. Billig. Up to now the three men had been across the room from her, but now Manning decided to move closer. He walked to the front of the room, and the teacher shrank back from him.

"Whose kids we got in here?" he asked.

"What do you mean?"

"These kids come from town? From farms? Ranches?"

"All of those," she said. "It's the only school in the county."

"So do we have some rich rancher's kid here?"

"You—I'm not going to tell you that." she said. "My God, you have your own child here?"

"That I do," Manning said, "and when I leave here, I'm takin' her with me. But until then, I need to know which of these kids is worth the most."

After a moment of silence, a voice from the back of the room said, "I reckon I am."

Chapter Twelve

It was very quiet outside the schoolhouse.

"Everybody's still at the fire," Crown commented.

"There's no reason for them to be out here," Clint said. "But if three men get out of there, you're going to need a posse."

"That's not an easy thing in this town," Crown said. "It's been a long time since I had to put together a posse. If it wasn't for you, I'd pretty much be alone in this."

"I could stay here and watch while you go to town for more men," Clint offered.

"They're still fightin' that fire," Crown said, "probably don't even know the bank's been hit."

"You could go back and tell them," Clint said. "I'll make sure these three don't leave here."

Crown thought it over.

"It ain't gonna hurt for me to try to get a posse together," he admitted.

"And if we can get them out of there before that, you won't need the posse."

"I'll be back shortly," Crown said. "Don't do nothin' stupid while I'm gone."

"Doing something stupid doesn't come natural to me," Clint said.

"And don't get killed."

"That's my specialty," Clint said, as Crown mounted up and headed back to town.

***

"One of 'em's leavin'," Bailey said.

"Which one?"

"I think the sheriff."

Manning moved back toward the windows, took a look outside.

"Why's he leavin' that one here?" he wondered. "Who is he?"

"He might be goin' back to town for a posse," Bailey suggested.

"They'll still be fightin' that fire," Manning said. "A posse ain't gonna be easy."

"Then we only have to deal with that one man," Bailey said. "Lyle and me, we can go out and take 'im."

Manning thought about it.

"How you gonna get out there?" he asked.

"Right out the door," Bailey said. "We'll surprise 'im and take 'im."

Manning looked at Victor.

"You good with that?" he asked.

"Whatever you say," Victor said. "I just wanna get away from here and split the money."

"Okay, then," Manning said, "try it." If they both got killed, he'd have all the money for himself. And he still had hostages.

"Let's go," Bailey said to Victor. "I'll go first, you follow."

"Got it."

They moved toward the door.

***

Clint had not been able to get a look at the rear of the schoolhouse but, in his experience, a small one like this wouldn't usually have a back door. If they were going to come out, they'd come out the front.

He retrieved the rifle that was on the horse, a service-able enough Winchester, and kept his eye on the front door. As it started to open, he fired as many shots as he could, quickly. He wanted to make sure he kept them inside.

***

The second Bailey touched the front door to crack it open, preparing to swing it wide, the shots rang out and lead began to strike the door.

He slammed the door shut quick and backed up. "Jesus!"

"Children," Mrs. Billig shouted, "on the floor. Get under your desks."

All of the kids ducked down.

It got quiet.

"What the hell was that?" Victor asked. "Five, six shots? I ain't never seen anybody fire a rifle that fast."

"Almost like he had a gatlin' gun," Bailey said.

"Get back to the windows!" Manning snapped. "That's no gatlin' gun, that's just a man who knows how to use a rifle."

"You have to get out of here!" Mrs. Billig shouted. "The children could get hurt. Your daughter could get hurt."

Manning looked at Linda, who was cowering beneath her desk.

"Linda, get up front by the teacher," he said. "Behind her desk."

The little girl ran to the teacher, who put her arms around her and drew her down behind the desk.

Some of the other kids started to get up to do the same.

"Nobody else!" Manning shouted. "Stay where you are, under your desks."

All the kids settled back down.

"All right," Manning said, "who was that said he was worth the most?"

"Me," a boy said.

"Stand up."

The boy did.

"How old are you?"

"Twelve."

"Why are you worth more?"

"Ma Pa's got a big ranch," he said, "and a lot of money."

"What's your Pa's name?"

"Harold Malcolm."

"What ranch?"

"The Big M."

"Where is it?"

"A few miles from here," the boy said. "I—I walk to school."

Manning looked at the teacher.

"Is he tellin' the truth?"

"No," she said, "he's lying."

Manning laughed.

"Why would he lie?" he asked. "I think you're the one who's lyin'." Manning looked at the boy. "You get to the front of the room, too, behind the teacher's desk. I don't want you catchin' a bullet."

"Who is this man?" Bailey asked, looking out the window.

Manning looked at him and said, "Let's find out."

Chapter Thirteen

Manning moved to the door and opened it a crack. "Don't shoot!" he yelled.

There were no shots.

"Who are you?" he called out and waited for an answer.

***

Clint reloaded the rifle from rounds he found in the saddlebags on the horse and waited. When the door opened again, he felt it wasn't for anyone to come out, so he held his fire.

"Don't shoot!" he heard. And then, "Who are you?"

"My name's Clint Adams!" he called back. "Who are you?"

"My name's Desmond Manning," the voice said. "Where's the sheriff?"

"He had to go back to the fire."

"I have fifteen children as hostages in here," Manning said.

"And is one of them yours?"

"Yes," Manning said. "My daughter. I just wanted to see her before I left."

"And now what?"

"And now I'm takin' her with me," Manning said.

"Do you expect me to just let you go?" Clint asked.

"Yes."

Some moments of silence went by, finally broken by Clint.

"All right."

"You'll do it?" Manning asked. "You'll let us go?"

"I will," Clint said, "just leave the child and the money behind."

He waited for an answer.

***

"He's the fuckin' Gunsmith!" Lyle Victor said, with more feeling than he'd spoken before.

"He expects us to leave the money?" Bailey asked.

Manning closed the door.

"He's the Gunsmith, damn it," Victor repeated.

"Shut up, Lyle!" Manning said. He looked around the room, saw that all eyes were on him.

"What are you going to do?" the teacher asked.

"I'm not sure," Manning said.

"Boss—" Bailey said.

Manning put his hand up.

"Just wait." He thought for a few minutes, his eyes darting about in his head. "Okay, I got it."

He opened the door slightly again.

"Adams!"

***

"Adams!" Clint heard.

"I'm here."

"We ain't leavin' the money," Manning shouted. "We'll be leavin' *with* the money, the teacher and my kid. We'll leave the other kids here."

"I can't agree to that," Clint called out. "We'll have to wait til the sheriff gets back. He makes the decisions."

"Oh yeah?" Manning said. "And he's gonna come back with a posse, ain't he? You better make the decision right now, or this teacher ain't gonna make it."

Clint thought fast. This was a way to get fourteen kids out of the schoolhouse safely. All he had to do was let them go with Manning's own child, and the teacher.

"Manning!"

"Yeah?"

"Leave the teacher," Clint said. "Take the money and your daughter."

He waited for a reply.

57

***

Manning slammed the door.

"That ain't bad," Bailey said. "At least we get the money, and you get your kid."

"We need a hostage they know we'll kill," Manning said. "They'd never think I'd kill my own kid—and I wouldn't."

"Let's take that boy," Bailey said. "The one who says his Pa's a big rancher."

"No!" Mrs. Billig shouted.

They all looked at her.

"Let me talk to this Clint Adams," she said. "I'll tell him I want to go with you."

"I like that idea. Come over here," Manning said.

She told the boy to stay behind the desk with Linda and walked over to Manning.

"You call out to Adams and tell him what you said," Manning told her. He cracked the door for her.

"Mr. Adams!" she called. "This is Jane Billig, the teacher."

***

Clint heard the teacher's voice. She sounded pretty strong.

"Are you all right?" he asked.

"I'm fine," she called back. "I'll go with them willingly, so they leave the other children."

"Is that the way you want it?" Clint asked.

"Yes, it is."

Clint gave it some quick thought. There was no telling when Sheriff Crown would be back. If he had a chance to save fourteen of the kids, he should probably take it.

"All right," he called out. "Manning?"

"Yeah, Adams," Manning said.

"You can take the money, the teacher and your daughter," Clint said. "But that's it."

He waited.

***

Manning slammed the door again, looked at the teacher.

"Get yourself and Linda ready."

She hurried across the room.

"We better get out of here while we can," Manning said to his men.

"You really think he's gonna let us go?" Bailey asked.

"We're gonna find out," Manning said.

Chapter Fourteen

Mrs. Billig instructed all the children to sit at their desks and wait for the sheriff to come in and get them.

Then she went to Linda, put her arm around her and walked her to the door.

"We're going with your Pa, honey," she said.

"But what about Momma?" the girl asked.

"You'll see your Momma, Linda," Mrs. Billig said. "You'll see her soon."

"Okay come on," Manning said, "it's time for us to go." He looked at his men. "Lyle, you go first, take the teacher, get her on your horse with you."

"Right, boss."

"Bailey, you take the money, and mount up. I'll take Linda on my horse with me."

"You don't think he's gonna try to stop us?" Bailey asked.

"Everythin' I've heard about the Gunsmith says he's a man of his word," Manning said.

"Looks like we'll find out," Bailey said.

***

As Clint watched, the door opened wide. First one man came out, with the teacher in front of him. A second man came out, carrying the bags of money from the bank. And then a third man came out, who he assumed was Manning. He was carrying a little girl.

All three men went to their horses and mounted up. Clint had to keep his word and let them ride off. Then he ran to the schoolhouse and entered, hoping to find that the fourteen kids were all right. He saw them all, sitting at their desks with their hands clasped on top.

"It's okay, kids," he said. "You're safe now."

"Are you the sheriff?" a boy of about twelve asked.

"No, but I'm working with him."

"Teacher told us not to move until the sheriff came," the boy said. The other children nodded, and none of them moved.

"Well then, that's what we'll do," Clint said. "We'll all just sit here until the sheriff gets here. How's that?"

All the children agreed.

Clint just hoped that when he told the sheriff the whole story, Ed Crown wouldn't hold it against him.

***

When Sheriff Crown arrived and saw the horses gone, he ran to the schoolhouse door and looked in. Clint was sitting at the teacher's desk and the children were seated at theirs.

"What the hell—" he said.

"Are you the sheriff?" the boy asked.

Crown came in so the boy could see his badge.

"That's right, I'm Sheriff Crown."

The boy looked relieved, and the other children began to move.

"Mrs. Billig said you'd send us home," the boy said.

"And I will," Crown said, "as soon as I get the whole story."

"I can tell it to you, Ed," Clint said. "Why don't you let these kids go home?"

"Okay, kids," Crown said, "get on home."

As the kids filed out, Crown grabbed the arm of the boy who had spoken.

"You're Hal Malcolm's kid, aren't you?"

"That's right."

"How do these smaller kids get home?"

"Me and some of the older ones walk them," the boy said.

"Okay," Crown said, releasing the boy's arm, "go ahead."

"Sheriff," he said, "I tol' them who I was, and that my Pa would pay. But they took the teacher and Linda, anyway. I—I tried to get them to take me, instead."

"You're a brave boy," Crown said. "Go on home."

"Yessir."

As the boy left, Crown walked to the front of the room.

"Where's the posse?" Clint asked.

"It's like I told you," Crown said. "They're too busy fightin' the fire. At least, that was their excuse."

"I get it."

"You wanna tell me what happened here?" Crown asked. "Why you let them go?"

"Sure, I'll tell you the whole story," Clint said. "Have a seat."

***

After Clint finished his story, Crown stared at him a few moments.

"Well?" Clint asked. "Say something. Yell at me."

"I guess you did what you thought was best," Crown said, finally. "You saved fourteen of the kids."

"I was hoping you'd feel that way."

"We're gonna have to go after 'em, you know," Crown said. "Get the money back."

"And the little girl."

"Was she really his?" Crown asked.

"I'd say yes, she was."

"I'm gonna have to tell the mother, then."

"Let's get back to town and return these horses," Clint said. "When we go after them, I'm going to want my own horse."

"I don't blame you for that."

As they left the schoolhouse, Crown said, "You know, folks already thought you was a hero, after what you did at the hotel. Now they're gonna be sayin' you saved the Children of Willow Springs."

Chapter Fifteen

When they got back to town, the hotel had pretty much burned to the ground. Clint's saddlebags and books had been inside. He had gotten out with the clothes on his back and his gun.

"We'll have to track them," Crown said on the way to his office, "and they'll know we're comin', so they won't make it easy."

"I'll trust you to track them, Ed," Clint said.

"I'm out of practice," Crown said, as they entered the office. "Do you want a gun from the rack?"

"My rifle was in the hotel," Clint said, "so yes, I'll need one."

"Take your pick."

Clint chose a shotgun, saw that he would have to clean it while they were on the trail.

Sheriff Crown chose a rifle.

"If you'll go to the livery to saddle your horse, you can tell Tad, the hostler, to saddle mine."

"And what will you be doing?"

"I've got to tell the mayor I'll be gone until we can return with the bank's money."

"Okay."

"And on the way out of town we'll have to stop and talk to the girl's mother," Crown said. "We can assure her we'll be bringin' her daughter back, and she can tell us everythin' she knows about the girl's father."

"That'll be good," Clint said. "We'll need all the background we can get on him so we know who we're dealing with."

"I'll meet you out front with the horses," Crown said. "I also have to tell Maggie I'm goin'. She won't be happy."

"She'll worry?"

"You've probably noticed she's younger than I am."

"I noticed."

"Well, she thinks I'm too old for this job, wants me to retire," Crown said. "If this hunt takes too damn long, I just might do it."

He left the office and headed for City Hall. Clint left only moments later for the livery stable.

***

"Oh!"

Manning heard the teacher yell and turned in time to see her fall from Victor's horse.

"What's wrong?" he asked.

She got to her feet, brushing off her bum, and glared.

"He put his hands on me," she said.

"I was tryin' to keep her from fallin' off," Victor said, with a smirk.

"It was . . . inappropriate."

"Teacher," Manning said, "would you rather walk? Actually, you'd have to run to keep up."

"I don't want to ride with him," she said, pointing.

"I'll take 'er," Bailey said, with a grin.

Manning rode over to Lyle Victor and abruptly handed him his daughter.

"Linda will ride with you," he said. "Make sure she doesn't fall off."

"Right, boss."

Then he rode over to the teacher and reached out his hand.

"You'll ride with me."

She studied Manning for a moment, suddenly aware of the fact that he was roughly handsome. He was also older and more mature than the other two.

"Very well," she said, reaching up.

He lifted her quite easily onto his horse, in front of him, so that when he took the reins up, his arms were around her. The of feel of him was disconcertingly thrilling.

"Okay?" he asked.

"Yes, fine."

"Then let's move."

He turned his horse and took the point.

Chapter Sixteen

Clint had his Tobiano and the sheriff's mare in front of the office when the sheriff returned.

"Okay," the lawman said, "I spoke with the mayor, and with Maggie. I left him considerably happier than she is."

They both mounted up.

"What about the girl's mother?" Clint asked.

"Her name's Diane Manning, lives on the outskirts of town. We'll stop on the way. The Mayor was nice enough to stop in and tell 'er what happened, and then told her to stay home and wait for me. There was no point in her going to the schoolhouse."

As they rode Clint said, "So, they're married."

"According to the mayor, they were," Crown said. "Not anymore. Apparently, Manning's a drunk who used to beat her. She was afraid for her child, so she threw him out. This is the first time he's been back in town in a few years. The mayor assumed he was here to try to see his daughter, not to rob the bank."

"I assume he decided to kill two birds with one stone, then," Clint said.

"I suppose so."

"Did the mayor know anything about the teacher?"

"Yes," Crown said. "She came with her husband from the East, but he died when they were here only four months. For the last few years, her life has been those kids she's teachin'."

"That explains why she went willingly," Clint said. "To safeguard the rest of her kids."

They reached the Manning house and dismounted.

"I think you should probably do the talking," Clint said to Crown, "since you're the official."

"Agreed."

They went to the front door and Crown knocked. The woman who opened the door was a brunette, lovely but harried-looking. Her eyes widened when she saw Crown's badge.

"Have you found her?" she demanded. "Did you bring her back?"

"Not yet, Ma'am," Crown said. "We're just on our way to track the robbers and get your daughter back, but we need some information."

"Information?"

"About your, uh, husband."

"Former husband," she corrected him. "I suppose you should come in."

They entered, but she stopped immediately and turned to face them, arms folded.

71

"You need to know that my former husband is a drunk, and he's dangerous," she said. "My daughter is in danger."

"Do you have any idea where your husband—former husband—might go now that he's got the bank's money."

"No, I don't—he robbed the bank?"

"And burned down a hotel," Clint added.

"Oh, I heard all the commotion," she said, "but I didn't connect it. So, he set fire to a hotel—"

"—to distract from the fact that he and his cohorts were robbin' the bank."

"And then he stopped at the schoolhouse to get my daughter?"

"That's how it looks," Crown said.

"And these two men with him," she asked, "Are they dangerous, as well?"

"There was some shootin' at the bank," Crown said, "and three people were killed."

"Oh, my God." She reached out for a chair and sat heavily in it.

"Now they're on the run and we're gonna track 'em."

"B-but why did you let them go?"

"It was a matter of saving the children in the schoolhouse, Ma'am," Clint said.

"Yes, of course," she said, "the other children. Are they all okay?"

"They're fine," Clint said.

"Did your—did Manning come here before he hit the bank and took your daughter?"

"Yes, he wanted to see Linda, but I kicked him out."

"It never occurred to you he might take her?" Clint asked.

"God help me, no," Diane said. "I don't think he really wants her. I think he's just gettin' back at me for ending' our marriage."

"He also took the teacher," Clint said. "Do you know her?"

"Not well," Diane said, "just to say hello to."

"Do you think he knew her?"

"No." Then her eyes widened. "Do you think she was helpin' him?"

"I'm just trying to get an idea of what we're dealing with," Clint said.

"You're dealiun' with a crazy drunk!" she snapped.

"Was he drunk when he came here?" Crown asked.

"N-no."

"And I don't think he was drunk when he hit the bank, or the schoolhouse," Crown said.

"It might be worse," Clint said, "that he's doing all of this when he's stone cold sober."

"Oh God . . ."

"Ma'am," Crown said, "we're gonna do our best to get your girl back."

"When?" she demanded.

"We're heading out right now," Clint said. "Sheriff Crown is an expert tracker. We'll catch up to them."

She wasn't looking particularly confident when they left.

Chapter Seventeen

When the riders cleared Willow Springs, Manning reined his horse in.

"Where are we headed, boss?" Bailey asked.

"I have a place in mind," Manning said. "You'll find out when we get there."

"When do we split the money?" Bailey asked.

"When we get there," Manning said.

"How long will that be?" Mrs. Billig asked.

"You don't get to ask questions, teacher," he said, into her hair. "Just sit there and smell nice."

She shivered from his breath on her and was surprised to find that it wasn't out of fear. She licked her lips because her mouth had gone dry.

Manning thought about having Bailey ride to check their back trail, but he had the money bags on his horse. He didn't want the man to be tempted. Of course, he could have had him hand the bags to Victor, but Manning didn't want those two to know he didn't trust them. He didn't trust anyone.

***

Crown and Clint picked up the trail left by the three horses from in front of the schoolhouse. They followed them out of town, and then for a few miles more before Crown stopped.

"Looks like they stopped here, but didn't dismount," he said. "They were probably deciding which way to go."

"I'd think a man like Manning would've had a plan," Clint commented.

"He might, who knows?" Crown said. "They're headed north, now."

"Do you have any idea what lies that way?" Clint asked.

"Sure, there are several towns over the next twenty miles, but I doubt they're headed there," Crown said. "It's just not far enough away, especially after burnin' down a hotel, kidnappin' a woman and child, robbin' the bank, and killin' three people."

"Agreed," Clint said. "Manning has got to have a destination in mind, one far enough away from where the crimes were committed."

"So we just have to keep following their trail," Crown said, "which means we're goin' north."

***

"We got about an hour before dark," Bailey said, looking at the sky as they rode. "Whataya wanna do, Des?"

"We'll ride for another hour, and then camp," Manning said. "I doubt they got a posse together quick in that town. And besides, they were still fightin' that fire."

"What about Adams?" Bailey asked.

"What about him?"

"You think he'd start trackin' us alone?"

"Seems to me he was workin' with the sheriff," Manning said. "That means he's probably gonna let that old lawman call the play. I don't think they're gonna catch up to us tonight. But we'll set watches anyway when we make camp, just in case."

***

As it started to get dark, they came across what looked like an old line shack.

"Let's camp here," Manning said.

"In the shack?" Bailey asked.

"You and Lyle outside," Manning said, "me and the teacher inside."

"What about your daughter?" Victor asked.

"She can sleep out under the stars with you guys," Manning said. "She gotta learn some time that you can't always be comfortable."

They dismounted. Victor took care of the horses, while Bailey built a fire. Manning took Jane Billig into the shack to have a look at it.

"This ain't so bad," he said to her. "What's your first name?"

"Jane."

"We're gonna sleep in here, Jane," he said. "But first you're gonna go out to that fire and cook us up some grub."

"Where will I get—"

"We've each got the makings in our saddlebags," Manning said. "Pans, coffee pot, beans, even some bacon. We were prepared to have to make camp."

"Mr. Manning," she said, "don't you think it would be better for Linda to sleep in here with us?"

"No," he answered. "Like I said, she's gotta learn some time. Now go out and start cookin'."

She obeyed, and before long they were sitting around the fire in the dark, eating. Jane kept Linda next to her, feeding her and trying to make the child feel as safe as she could.

"Bailey," Manning said, when the meal was over, "you take the first watch—and keep an eye on my daughter. Lyle, you're next, and then you knock on the shack door to wake me. Got it?"

"Got it, boss," Lyle Victor said.

Jane talked softly to Linda to get her to feel secure, even while lying outside on the ground near those two men. After that she followed Manning into the shack, knowing what was coming and—in spite of herself—feeling thrilled by it.

There was an old cot in the shack, but it was only for one person. Manning spread a blanket out on the floor next to it, then sat on it and looked at Jane.

"You're very pretty, you know," he said.

"Thank you."

"You know why we're in here, right?"

"I have an idea."

"Do you want to scream?" he asked. "Or run?"

She hesitated, then said, "No."

"Let your hair down."

She reached behind her head to unpin her hair, and it fell past her shoulders.

"Now that's better," he said. "If I had a teacher who looked like you, I'd've stayed in school."

She stood in front of him with her hands behind her back.

"Now take off that dress and come over here," he said. "I need help gettin' undressed . . ."

***

Clint and Crown decided to make camp.

"No point riskin' our horses by ridin' at night," Crown said.

"Agreed."

"I'll take care of the horses," the lawman said, "and you build the fire."

"Right."

Crown had the wherewithal to pack a frying pan and a coffee pot in his saddlebags, giving Clint some cans of beans to put in his.

"Coffee and beans are all I've ever needed on the trail," Crown said, as they ate.

"It gets old after a while," Clint said, "that's why I like to have some bacon, beef jerky, and lately the makings of some johnnie cakes."

"We left with a little short notice for all that," Crown said.

"You're right," Clint said. "Coffee and beans are fine for this hunt."

"I feel sorry for that little girl, and the teacher," Crown said, "being dragged all over creation by a crazy man."

"A crazy man who happens to be the girl's father," Clint pointed out.

"But if her mother's right, he didn't really want the child," Crown said. "He's just lookin' to hurt the mother."

"And doing a pretty good job of it," Clint said. "But I'm also worried about the teacher. There's no telling what those three could be doing to the poor woman."

***

Jane Billig undressed slowly, partially from shyness, and partially from a desire to inflame Manning's interest.

While he watched, Manning removed his boots, and his shirt. He stopped when she got to the point of being fully naked. As she let her dress drop to the floor, he caught his breath. This teacher was in her thirties and had the full body of a woman who belonged in bed. Her breasts were large with heavy undersides, her hips and butt were built wide for a man's comfort.

"That's what I've been waitin' for," he said to her. "Come on over here."

As she approached him, he removed his trousers and tossed them aside. When his hard cock jutted up at her from his crotch, she realized it had been a long time for her—a very long time.

Chapter Eighteen

For the next hour it was forgotten that Manning was a kidnapper and Jane was his victim. They rolled about on the blanket as first he roamed her body with his hands and mouth, and then she took the initiative, pushed him down on his back and gave her attention to his hard penis.

"That's it, that's it," he said, as she ran her mouth and tongue over it.

"Mmmmm," she moaned, with her mouth full. She began to suck him, bobbing her head up and down until he reached down to free himself from her mouth and pull her up onto him.

"Come on, baby," he said, "ride it."

She lifted her hips, and since her pussy was already running and wet, she slid right down on his pole.

"Ah, yeahhhh . . ." he gasped.

She began to slide up and down on him, concerned with nothing but the sensation of his cock inside her. They went on like that for a while until, abruptly, he grabbed her hips and reversed their positions without losing contact with her. He took her legs in his hands, spread her wide and began to fuck her with more diligence.

She groaned and moaned every time he drove himself into her, and that, combined with his grunts, was pretty loud . . .

***

Bailey, still on the first watch, heard grunts and groans. He also swore he could see the shack moving, shaking. It wasn't hard to figure out what was going on inside.

He looked over at the little girl, who seemed sound asleep, wrapped in a blanket. Lying next to her, also fast asleep, was Lyle Victor, who hadn't moved or made a sound since he turned in.

The two bags of bank money were sitting on the other side of the fire. He had put them there so he could keep his eye on them. Now he wondered, if he saddled his horse and rode off with those bags, would anybody even notice til morning? There was certainly enough money in those bags to be cut up into three very nice shares—but the whole amount for one man was tempting. Of course, if he did that, not only would the law be after him, but so would Des Manning.

Rather than steal the money, he poured himself another cup of coffee and watched the shack continue to shake.

***

"Oh God," Jane said, as Manning pulled his cock from her and laid down beside her. "You never know you needed something until you finally get it."

"I know what you mean, teacher," he said. "I knew you wanted this from the moment I first saw you."

"How could you have?" she asked, breathlessly. "I didn't know, not until . . ."

"Until when?"

"Until you pulled me up on your horse, and I felt your body against mine."

"Yeah, I felt somethin', too," he said. What he didn't tell her was that all he felt was his penis swelling as *her* body pressed against *his*.

She rolled over and put her head on his shoulder.

"You know," she said, "I've been lost for years, ever since my husband died. But now, with you, I think I may have found myself, again."

"Is that right?"

"Yes," she said, running her hand down his stomach to his crotch, where she fondled him. "I do. So, where will we be going after tonight?"

He caught his breath as she began to stroke him.

"We don't have to talk about that right now," he said. "After all, we're not finished for tonight, are we?"

She slithered to press his hard penis to her cheek and said, "Not finished, at all . . ."

***

Lyle Victor knocked tentatively on the door of the shack. When Bailey woke him, he told the young man what was going on in the shack.

"You're kiddin'," Victor said.

"Why do you think he took her in there with him and not his daughter?" Bailey asked.

"I try not to think, Bailey," Victor said. "I just do what I'm told."

So, as he had been told, he was waking Manning up for his watch. He just hoped he wasn't interrupting anything.

When the door opened, Manning stepped right out.

"Your watch, boss," he said.

"I got it, Lyle," Manning said. "You go back to sleep."

"Yes, sir."

"Lyle?"

"Yes, sir?"

"Where's the money."

"Bailey is sleepin' with it, sir," Victor said. "I don't think he trusts us."

"He's a smart man not to trust anybody, Lyle," Manning said. "See you in a few hours."

"'night, boss."

Manning walked over to where Bailey was sleeping, with his arms wrapped around the money bags. Then he checked on his daughter. She was also sound asleep.

He went over to the fire and poured himself a cup of hot coffee.

***

By the time Manning woke Bailey, Victor and Linda, he had already doused the campfire and saddled the horses.

"What about breakfast?" Victor asked.

"Have some beef jerky," Manning said. "We'll eat on the move."

They mounted up. This time Manning had Linda on his horse with him.

"But . . . what about the teacher?" Bailey asked, looking over at the shack.

"Let her sleep," Manning said. "We don't need her, anymore."

Chapter Nineteen

When Clint woke Crown the next morning, he already had a pot of coffee going, and a pan of johnnie cakes.

"I told you," Clint said, "lately I travel with the makings."

They drank the coffee, ate the cakes and discussed their day.

"They have about a six-hour head start on us," Clint said. "And traveling with a woman, a child, and only three horses, we should be catching up to them."

"And they would've also camped for the night," Crown said. "They wouldn't take a chance on a horse goin' lame."

"So if we pushed," Clint said, "we can close the gap."

"And what do we do when we catch up to them?" Crown asked. "They're still gonna have two hostages to hide behind."

"I suggest when we do catch up, we keep trailing them," Clint said, "and wait for the right moment to move."

"Sounds like a plan," Crown said. "Let's get mov-in'."

They doused the fire, each saddled their own horse and headed out at double the pace.

***

"Whataya think?" Crown asked.

"Looks like an old line shack," Clint said.

Crown looked around, then down at the ground again.

"The tracks seem to lead right to it," he admitted.

"Doesn't appear like anybody's there now," Clint said, "but we might as well take a look."

They urged their horses on and approached the shack slowly.

"There was a campfire here last night," Clint said, pointing. "They were here."

They both dismounted and Crown went and put his hand on the remnants of the fire.

"It's cold," he said.

"They're still hours ahead of us."

"We better get movin' then," Crown said, starting to mount up.

"Wait," Clint said. "I think we should take a look in the shack."

"What for?"

"Maybe he left the little girl behind."

"Why would he?" Crown asked. "It's his daughter."

"A daughter Diane Manning said he didn't really want," Clint reminded him.

"You don't think she's dead, do you?"

"Only one way to find out."

Crown dropped his horse's rein to the ground and followed Clint to the shack.

"There's footprints here," Clint said, pointing to the dirt in front of the door. "Two, maybe three people."

"So somebody slept in the shack," Crown said, "and somebody outside by the fire. Probably standin' watch."

"Probably watching for us," Clint said.

They approached the door, which was ajar, and pushed it wide open.

"Oh Lord," Crown said.

There was a naked woman lying on a blanket in the middle of the floor.

"Do you think—" Crown started.

"Looks like her."

Clint walked to the body. The woman was extremely well-endowed, and extremely dead. Clint knew that even before he leaned over her.

"Is she dead?" Crown asked.

"Yes."

"How?"

"Strangled." Clint looked at Crown. "I only saw her from afar. Is this the teacher?"

Crown leaned over to have a look.

"Yeah, that's her," he said, shaking his head. "Jane Billig. Poor woman."

Both men instinctively looked around them, hoping against hope not to find the dead body of a little girl in there, as well.

"She ain't here," Crown said.

"They must have decided they didn't need the teacher, anymore," Clint said.

"So they raped 'er and killed 'er?"

Clint looked around again, found the woman's dress and picked it up.

"From the tracks outside, I don't think all the men were in here," he said. "And this dress isn't torn."

"You don't think she was raped?" Crown asked. "They could've told her to take the dress off."

"Rapists aren't usually polite, and they don't wait," Clint said.

"You got a point."

"She could've taken the dress off willingly for several reasons," Clint said. "She could've just been trying to save her life, or maybe . . ."

"Maybe what?"

"Maybe she just wanted to," Clint said.

***

They took the time to bury Jane Billig in a clearing near the shack. They had to scrape out a shallow grave with their hands, and then cover it with rocks.

"I'm sorry to have to leave her here," Crown said, "we've got one more reason to keep goin'."

"Maybe we can pick her up on the way back and take her to town," Clint said. "Did she have any family?"

"Only those kids in the school," Crown told him. "They were her family."

"They're going to be crushed," Clint said. "Maybe if I hadn't let them go-p—"

"Hey," Crown said, cutting him off, "this wasn't your fault. You did what you had to do to save those kids. But we got one more to save."

"You're right."

They walked to their horses, quenched their thirst with some water, and remounted.

"Let's get those bastards," Clint said.

Chapter Twenty

Since they didn't have the teacher to worry about anymore, Manning decided to send Lyle Victor to check their back trail.

"If we're bein' hunted, I wanna know how much of a head start we have on them," he told Victor. "And don't let 'em see you."

"Don't worry, boss, I won't."

As Victor rode away, Bailey said, "You really think he's up to that?"

"Maybe," Manning said, "maybe not. If they catch him, we'll only have to cut the money two ways, not three."

"And when do we do that?"

"As soon as we get where we're goin'," Manning said. "When we're safe."

"And how much further is that?"

"First let's find out if there's a posse," Manning said, "or just two men, the sheriff and the Gunsmith. We can worry about splittin' the money up later."

Bailey put his hands on the money bags, which were draped over his saddle. As long as he was holding them, he was willing to wait.

***

"Pa, can we go home now?"

Manning looked down at the little girl who was sitting in front of him on his horse.

"We're goin' home, honey."

"I mean home to Ma."

"Your Ma don't want you no more," he told her.

"What?" She began to cry. He put one arm around her and hugged her to him.

"That's okay, Linda," he said. "I want you."

"You d-do?" she stammered.

"Yes, I do," Manning said, patting her. "Now shut up until I tell you to talk."

She started to cry again, softly.

***

"I'm going to keep my eyes straight ahead," Clint said to Crown as they rode along. "I suggest you look around."

"What are you expectin'?" Crown asked. "An ambush?"

"That's always possible," Clint said, "but they might also send one rider to check their back trail. At least, that's what I'd do."

"Makes sense," Crown said. "They're gonna wanna know how many men are pursuing them."

"How are they going to react to just two?" Clint asked.

"I guess that depends on whether or not they know one of the men is you."

"Good point, I suppose. Let's just keep alert."

***

Lyle Victor had an idea.

Manning told him to just watch, but he didn't think his boss would complain if he fixed it so they weren't being followed. So his intention was to see who was hunting them, and then bushwhack them.

He rode back only a few miles and decided he would just settle in and wait. He found a likely high spot, dismounted, got down on his belly. If there were two of them, he could take care of them both. If there was a posse, then he'd pick off the sheriff. The posse wouldn't be the same without the sheriff to lead them.

Victor was a young, impetuous man in his twenties who usually did whatever Manning told him to do. But now he was thinking it was time for him to step up and make a decision for himself.

***

"What is it?" Sheriff Crown asked as Clint reined in the Tobiano.

"Instinct," Clint said, "nothing more."

There were high bluffs up ahead that they had to pass through.

"This is just too good a spot for an ambush to pass up," Clint said. "And we haven't seen a rider checking their back trail, like I expected."

They sat still on their horses and stared ahead.

"How do you wanna play this?" Crown asked.

"If we try to go around, we're going to lose ground," Clint said. "I think we have to go through and deal with whatever comes."

"Easy for you to say," Crown said. "I'm the easiest target with the sun reflecting off this badge on my chest."

"That's easy," Clint said. "Take it off and put it in your pocket."

"Good idea," Crown said, and did it. "Now what?"

"Now we each have a fifty-fifty chance of getting shot."

"Somehow," Crown said, "that don't make me feel any better about this."

"Okay," Clint said, "Let me think."

Chapter Twenty-One

Lyle Victor was starting to get nervous. It was getting later in the day, and he still didn't see anyone on the trail. Could it be possible they weren't being hunted? Was he waiting here for nothing? And he couldn't stay up here once it got dark.

He was growing more and more uncomfortable, his hands were sweating as he held his rifle tightly, despite the cold. The sweat from his brow dripped into his eyes, burning them.

***

Clint and Crown decided to chance losing some ground, in favor of safety.

"I'll go around," Clint said. "Give me ten minutes, then start riding, slowly."

"All right," Crown said.

"If someone's waiting to ambush us, I might be able to surprise them."

"Let's hope so," Crown said.

"Remember," Clint said. "Ten minutes,"

"Are you sure about this?" Crown asked.

"No," Clint said, "I'm not. As I said, it's a matter of instinct, but mine has never let me down."

"Let's get to it, then," Crown suggested.

Clint dismounted, handed the Tobiano's reins to Crown, and then continued quickly on foot. By his reckoning, he had been moving for about eight minutes when he saw it—a horse, tied to a tree. He approached it, saw that there was no rifle in the scabbard. It seemed as if his instinct was correct. He looked up toward the top of the bluff, then started to ascend.

***

"It's gettin' dark," Manning said to Bailey. "Let's camp here and give Lyle a chance to catch up."

They dismounted, and he put Linda down on the ground. She stood still and waited.

"I'll get a fire goin'," Manning said. "We can have somethin' hot waitin' for Lyle when he gets here. He's gonna be cold."

"*I'm* cold, Pa," Linda said.

"I'm gonna wrap you in a blanket," he told her. "You'll be nice and warm."

"I'll see to the horses," Bailey said.

"Good."

By the time Bailey had unsaddled and picketed the horses, Manning had wrapped his little girl in a blanket, gotten the fire going, and had a pot of coffee on the fire.

"Pa, I'm hungry," Linda whined.

"Don't whine," he told her. "We'll all eat when Lyle gets back. Now just be still!"

"Yes, Pa."

Manning thought Victor had already been gone too long. Something was wrong. The young man had gotten himself into trouble or made a bad decision. Or perhaps his horse had gone lame. Whatever happened, if he didn't make it back, there would only be two shares of the money, as he had told Bailey. And if he did get back, and brought with him some information about their pursuers, they would be no worse off than they had been before.

In truth, Manning would have been very happy to have Lyle Victor just disappear.

***

Clint saw the man lying atop the bluff with his rifle. As he had thought, the man was set for an ambush. Then he heard Sheriff Crown with both horses, and saw the man lean into his rifle.

***

Just when Lyle Victor was about to give up, he heard the horses. He leaned forward, into his rifle, sighted down the barrel and waited. When the two horses came into view, he realized one horse did not have a rider.

Shit, he thought.

"Just stand easy," A voice said, from behind him. "Let the rifle go."

Victor stiffened.

"Don't even think about it," Clint advised, seeing the man tense up. He knew he was thinking about whirling around and firing his rifle.

"Are you the Gunsmith?" the man asked.

"That's me."

Clint thought it might be enough to keep the man from trying something, but he didn't realize he was dealing with a headstrong young man. Lyle Victor was thinking, this was his chance to make a name for himself.

He turned, bringing his rifle around quickly . . .

Chapter Twenty-Two

Sheriff Crown watched from below as the man he would later find out was called Lyle Victor fell from atop the bluff after a single gunshot.

He rode over to the fallen man, dismounted, checked him and then looked up to see Clint looking down at him.

"He's dead," he called out.

"He didn't give me a choice," Clint called back. "I'll be right down."

While he waited for Clint, Crown went through the man's pockets. When Clint arrived, he had the man's horse with him.

"I went through his saddlebags," Clint said. "There's nothing to indicate he's one of the bank robbers."

"I went through his pockets," Crown said. "Same here. But why else would he be waitin' to bushwhack us?"

"He might've just been after me," Clint said.

"Naw," Crown said, "too much of a coincidence. He's one of 'em."

"If so, then, they're down to two," Clint said.

"And a child," Crown reminded him.

"Right."

"I guess we should bury him," Crown said.

"You know what?" Clint said. "He was going to ambush us, probably shoot us in the back. I don't think he deserves to be buried."

"Whatayou wanna do with him?" Crown asked.

"I say let's just push him by the wayside and keep on going."

"Fine with me," Crown said. "And the horse?"

"We'll unsaddle it and let it go loose. We don't have time to find it a home."

They shoved the man's body aside, unsaddled the horse and set it free, then mounted up and started off again.

"Uh-oh," Crown said, after a few miles.

"What?" Clint asked.

"I just took a look behind us," Crown said. "We've got company."

Clint turned and saw the horse they had set free. The animal was following them. Some horses, once domesticated, simply couldn't be without people. This one, which looked like a 5 or 6-year-old dun, seemed to be one of those.

They stopped and the horse came right up to them, stared at them.

"What do we do with him?" Crown asked.

"Nothing," Clint said. "Just let him follow. If we come to a town, we can turn him over to a livery stable."

And so they continued on, with the dun following close behind.

***

"Pa," Linda said, "I have to wee."

"Bailey," Manning called, as the man was riding up ahead of them. It was the next morning and Lyle Victor still hadn't caught up to them.

"Yeah?"

"I gotta stop for the girl."

"Why?"

"She's gotta go," Manning said.

"Then she better go," Bailey said.

Manning dismounted, took the girl down from the horse, then walked her to a space between two rocks that were bigger than she was.

"You can do it here," he told her. "Make sure you take your bloomers down, and don't get 'em wet."

"Yes, Pa."

Manning left her and walked over to where Bailey was waiting.

"You know," the man said, "I'm thinkin' maybe we should split the money and go our separate ways from here."

"Why's that?"

"Well, you got the girl and she's slowin' us down," Bailey said.

"If you wanna go on ahead, you can," Manning said.

"We could each take a bag—"

"I'll take both bags," Manning said. "We can meet later for a split."

"Now wait," Bailey said. "That ain't what I meant."

"Well," Manning said, "if we each take a bag, one might have more in it than the other, don't you think?"

"Maybe—"

"And since you been luggin' them around, you probably have an idea which one has more."

"I don't really—I guess we should stay together, then," Bailey said.

"Good idea," Manning said.

"I'm finished, Pa," the girl said.

Manning looked at her, saw that her bloomers were down around her ankles.

"Pull those up," he snapped.

"I can't," she whined.

Manning looked at Bailey, who looked away. The man went over to his daughter, crouched down and pulled up her bloomers.

"There," he said, standing, "now let's get movin', again."

Chapter Twenty-Three

"I don't believe it," Crown said.

"What?" Clint reined in the Tobiano and looked back at the lawman.

"My horse is lame," Crown said.

Abruptly, he dismounted, lifted the horse's left foreleg.

"Is it bad?" Clint asked.

"His ankle's swollen," Crown said. "He can walk, but he can't carry me."

The two men looked at each other, then at the loose horse that had been following them for miles.

"I'll put my saddle on that one," Crown said. "It won't take long. Then we can lead mine until we come to a town, or a ranch, where we can leave 'im."

"You unsaddle yours, and I'll bring the dun over."

Clint walked over to the dun, who stood still and watched him.

"I guess you're going to come in handy after all aren't you fella?" Clint asked, stroking the dun's neck. "Come on."

He led the horse over to where Crown was waiting and watched while his friend saddled the animal.

"How does he feel?" Clint asked, when Crown mounted up.

"A bit more barrel-chested than mine," Crown said, "but he feels good."

They didn't have an extra bridle for Crown's horse, so they would just have to hope that he—like the loose horse—would follow them.

"He moves well, too," Crown said, after a few miles.

"That's good," Clint said. "There's a town up ahead."

"There's no rush to get rid of my horse."

"No, I mean we can check and see if they stopped for supplies," Clint said, "and also find someplace to leave your horse."

"Oh," Crown said, "I suppose you're right. There's no point in lettin' my horse slow us down."

"I didn't say—"

"You didn't have to," Crown said. "I've seen the way you treat your horses."

"It's just that I don't own my animals," Clint explained. "It's more like we're . . . partners."

"All right, then," Crown said. "We'll drop him off first chance we get."

The ground was hard in many places, and they'd had to pick up the trail again a few times because of that. If the two men stopped off in a town, people would remember them, because of the little girl.

Clint hoped the little girl would be all right. Granted she was with her father, but according to her mother, he didn't really want her.

"What're you thinkin' about?" Crown asked. "You look like you lost your best friend, or somethin'."

"I'm thinking about the kid," Clint said. "I keep hoping we don't come across her body somewhere along here."

"You think he'd do that to his own daughter?" the lawman asked.

"I don't know," Clint said. "He's a killer, we know that. And her mother said he didn't really want the girl."

"Yes, but to kill 'er —"

"I know," Clint said. "He'd have to be some kind of monster. But we don't know the man, do we?"

"I suppose not," Crown agreed.

"She's bound to slow them down eventually," Clint said. "Then what will he do?"

"Maybe he'll just drop her off somewhere along the way," Crown said, "like we're gonna do to my horse."

"That would be best," Clint said. "For the girl, I mean. That'd be the best thing for all of us."

Chapter Twenty-Four

"Why here?" Bailey asked, early the next day.

Manning pointed up ahead.

"It's a small town, but we need supplies. It should have what we need, and a town like this won't have law we have to dodge."

"You don't think so?"

"I know so."

"And what about . . . the girl?"

"What about her?" Manning asked.

"This could be a place to leave her."

"Why would I wanna leave 'er?" Manning asked. "She's my kid."

"I thought you only took her to get back at your wife," Bailey said.

"You mean my ex-wife."

"Yeah, but—"

"And did I ever say that?" Manning asked, looking down at the child seated in front of him.

"Well, no, but—"

"Don't worry about her," Manning said. "She's my problem. We'll just ride in, pick up some things, and ride out again."

"Whatever you say."

"And maybe Lyle'll catch up."

"If he hasn't by now," Bailey said, "I don't think he will."

***

The town was called Little Journey. There were only a few buildings, but one of them was a trading post.

Manning and Bailey dismounted in front.

"I'll go in and get the supplies," Manning said "You stay out here with Linda. Don't let her wander off."

"I won't."

As Manning went inside, Bailey crouched down in front of the girl.

"Do you like ridin' with your Pa?"

"No," she said. "I wanna go home to my Ma."

"You'll go home soon," Bailey said to her. "I'm sure of it."

"But when?"

"Oh . . . as soon as he gets tired," Bailey said.

"Tired?" she asked. "Of what?"

Of you, he wanted to say, but changed his mind.

"Don't you worry about it."

A middle-aged woman came out of the trading post, stopped when she saw Linda.

"What a lovely little girl," the woman said, leaning over Linda. "Is she yours?"

"No," Bailey said, "I wouldn't know what to do with a little girl."

"I would," the woman said, touching Linda's face, her long blonde hair. "Oh, I would, indeed."

She smiled at Linda and walked on.

Linda was sitting on the edge of the boardwalk, Bailey standing in front of her, when Manning came out. When Bailey saw the look on Manning's face, he wondered if the man was hoping he *would* have let her wander off.

"Everythin' okay out here?" he asked.

"Oh, sure, everythin's fine," Bailey said. "Some woman wanted to take 'er, but I didn't let 'er. That was my job, right?"

"That's right."

Manning went to his horse, stuffed his purchases into his saddlebags, then turned to Linda.

"Ready to go?"

"Pa," she asked, as he lifted her up, "are you tired, yet?"

"Why do you ask?" he replied, putting her on the horse and then climbing up behind her.

"That other man said I could go home to Ma when you got tired," she answered.

"He did, huh? Well, we'll see, won't we . . ."

The two men and the little girl rode out of Little Journey . . .

***

"I've always wondered where some towns get their names," Sheriff Crown said, as they sat in front of the rotting signpost. "Little Journey."

"Do you know anything about it?" Clint asked.

"Not a thing."

"Well, if we're on the trail any longer, we're going to need some coffee and beef jerky. We might as well stop there, see if they did the same thing. Maybe we can also leave your horse with somebody."

"Why not?" Crown said. "The trail keeps goin' in and out. If somebody saw 'em, it'd be helpful to know we're still goin' the right way."

"Okay, fine," Clint said. "Then Little Journey here we come."

Chapter Twenty-Five

Clint and Crown rode into Little Journey at dusk.

"There ain't much here," Crown observed.

"There's a store," Clint said. "That's all we need."

They reined in their horses in front of the trading post and went inside. Clint went to the counter and told the man he needed coffee and beans.

"I just got some canned peaches in, if you're interested," the clerk said.

"Add a couple of cans," Crown said, from behind Clint. "That sounds good."

As Clint was settling up, he asked, "Have you seen two men with a little girl sometime today?"

"There was a man here, buying supplies," the clerk said. "He didn't have a small child with him, but I did see another man waiting outside with a little blonde girl."

"Do you have any idea where they were going from here?" Clint asked.

"Not a clue," the clerk said. "This ain't much of a town, but I do get lots of customers in here from the surrounding area. I'm afraid I got busy after he settled up with me and left with his purchases."

"Okay, thanks."

"Hold on," the clerk said, as Clint and Crown were leaving.

"What is it?" Clint asked.

"I had a customer right before him, Mrs. Howard. I thought I saw her speaking to the child after she left here."

"Where would we find her?" Clint asked.

***

The woman, Mrs. Howard, ran one of the other businesses in town, a small café at the far end of the street.

"We might as well have something to eat while we're here," Clint said at the door. "We'll have to camp outside of town."

"Sounds good to me."

They entered the empty café and sat at a table. A middle-aged woman came up to them and smiled.

"Can I help you gentlemen?" she asked.

"Are you Mrs. Howard?" Clint asked.

"Yes, I am," she said. "Did someone send you?"

"The clerk over at the trading post," Clint said. "We're looking for two men traveling with a little girl. The clerk said you might have seen them."

"I did see a man and a darling little girl," she said.

"When was it?" Crown asked.

115

"Earlier today." She noticed the badge on his shirt. "Are they in trouble?"

"They robbed a bank and kidnapped the girl," Clint said. "We're trying to get her back to her mother."

"You know," the woman said, "she did look like a sad little thing."

"Would you happen to know which way they went when they left?" Clint asked. "Or perhaps you heard them say where they were headed?"

"No," she said, "the man with her was very unpleasant. I got the distinct impression he wasn't happy about having the little girl with him. Is he her father?"

"One of the two men is her father," Clint said. "I don't know which one you encountered."

"Well, I hope he wasn't her father," she said. "Can I get you gents something to eat?"

"Two steak dinners," Crown said. "Please."

"Comin' up," she said. "I'm sorry I don't have any beer, but I can offer you water or coffee?"

"I'll take water," Crown said, "and my friend, here, likes strong coffee."

"That's the only way I make it," she said. "I'll be right back."

As she walked away Crown said, "Sounds like the man she saw with the little girl wasn't her father."

"No," Clint said, "he must've been in the store."

"I guess we better keep headin' north," Crown said. "We'll pick up the trail again."

"When the lady comes back, we'll get an idea of how far ahead of us they are," Clint said.

"And of how good a cook she is."

***

The steaks were perfectly cooked, and Clint's coffee was good and strong.

When she brought them each a slice of pie for dessert Crown asked, "Why is this place so empty. You're one helluva cook, Ma'am."

"It's breakfast time that we get a crowd," she said. "They come in from all over the county. But most of the folks stay home for supper."

"Their loss," Clint said.

While they were settling their bill Clint asked, "What time was it when you saw the man with the little girl, Mrs. Howard?"

"Oh, that was this afternoon," she said. "Must've been one or two."

As they left the café Crown said, "That puts them a good six hours ahead of us."

"Shouldn't change overnight," Clint said. "They'll camp, we'll camp as soon as we get outside of town."

"Hey, that means we could come back and be part of the breakfast crowd."

"I don't know about you these days, Ed," Clint said, "but I don't like crowds."

"Nah," Crown said, "you're right. Can't say much for them myself. Now that I got me a wife, I eat most of my meals home, too."

"You're a lucky man," Clint said. "If I haven't told you that, yet."

"I know it," Crown said. "I got a younger wife who can cook. What more could I ask for?"

"Retirement?" Clint asked, as they mounted up.

"That might be just the thing, after this is all over," Crown admitted. "Sure would make Maggie—and my old bones—happy."

"Well," Clint said, "I'll bet there's nothing like a younger wife who can cook, and who's happy."

Chapter Twenty-Six

The next morning Manning and Bailey had bacon and coffee for breakfast.

"Probably should've got some milk for the kid," Bailey said.

"And have it go sour on the trail," Manning said, looking over at Linda as she nibbled on some bacon. "She'll make do with water."

"You know," Bailey said, "that lady in town would take her. We could still go back and drop 'er off."

"One," Manning said, holding up one finger, "I ain't lookin' to drop 'er off anywhere, and two, we head back we're liable to run into a posse. Or, at least, a lawman and the Gunsmith."

"I'm guessin' Lyle ran into them and didn't come out on top," Bailey said.

"Then he's an idiot," Manning said. "I told him just to watch."

"Yeah, but you knew he'd try somethin' and get himself killed," Bailey said. "Come on, Des. That's why you sent him, ain't it?"

"You gonna complain about a two-way split, Bailey?" Manning asked.

"I sure ain't."

"There ya go, then," Manning said.

"But I didn't sign on to be a babysitter."

"No problem," Manning said. "I'll be watchin' her myself from now on."

"Good," Bailey said, and I'll keep an eye on these money bags."

"You do that, Bailey," Manning said. "You just keep doin' that."

***

As planned, Clint and Crown camped just outside of town. Since they'd eaten well at the café, they built the fire and only put a pot of coffee on it.

Seated at the fire, Crown looked across at Clint and said, "It's been a while for me. Ain't been out on the trail in years."

"How's your backside from the time in the saddle?" Clint asked.

"Gettin' back in shape," Crown said. "I did spend a lot of years in the saddle before I settled in Willow Springs, remember."

"I do remember," Clint said. "I was on the trail with you plenty of times."

"And when do you intend to settle down?" Crown asked.

"How about never?" Clint replied.

"Why not?"

"I'm a little too old to be changing my ways."

"That's what I thought, but I'm plenty older than you," Crown said. "Maggie's changed me, and it's been for the better."

"I'm happy for you, Ed," Clint said, "but it just isn't going to happen for me."

"Well, Maggie's gonna give it a good try," Crown warned him. "She's got a few friends she's lookin' to introduce you to."

"By the time we're done with this little task, I'm going to be ready to move on," Clint said. "She's going to have to try to match her friends up with somebody else, I'm afraid. I'm just not in the market."

"When we get back," Crown said, "I'll let you tell 'er that."

Chapter Twenty-Seven

By midday the following day, Clint thought they should have closed the gap between themselves and the two outlaws. But they had reached a point where the trail seemed to have dried up.

"What the hell happened?" Crown asked. "We've been managing to find the trail again. Why not now?"

"Could be one of two reasons," Clint said. "Either they brushed the tracks away, or they changed direction and we didn't catch it."

"So I guess we'll have to go back to the last point where we saw the tracks, and see what we missed," Crown said.

"You know," Clint said, "brushing tracks away with some branches can leave its own kind of trail."

"So you think we should look for brush marks?"

"I think we should give that a try before we turn around and go back, costing us time."

"We'll have to move slower," Crown said. "That's gonna cost us time, anyway."

"There's not much more we can do."

"Okay, then," Crown said, "since I've been off the trail for so long, you take the lead."

"Right."

***

Manning and Bailey reined in their horses and removed the branches they had been dragging along behind them.

"You think that's gonna do it?" Bailey asked, as he and Manning tossed the branches aside.

"Maybe not," Manning said. "They might be able to detect the brush marks, but I'm just lookin' to give us a little more time."

"Time for what?"

"For our next stop," Manning said.

"And where's that gonna be? We're gettin' pretty close to Omaha. We ain't goin' there, are we?"

"No," Manning said, "no place as big as Omaha, or Lincoln, or even Council Bluffs."

"Then where?"

"We're goin' to a town called Cornville."

"I never heard of it," Bailey said.

"And I'm sure the lawman and Adams ain't, neither."

"And what's there?"

"I got a lady waitin' for me there," Manning said, "and that's where we're gonna divvy up the money."

"About time, too."

***

They crossed a stream and Crown shook his head.

"If they followed this stream for a while, we'll never find the trail."

"They've been heading north," Clint said. "This stream goes east to west. If they used it, they didn't use it for long. You go east, I'll go west. Maybe one of us will find their trail coming out of the stream. Whoever finds it can fire one shot and then wait for the other to catch up."

"Okay," Crown said, "but I'm thinkin' we're gonna end up turnin' back."

"Keep a sharp eye out, Ed," Clint said. "Let's cross that bridge if and when we come to it."

They both turned their horses and headed off in opposite directions, riding in the stream.

It took only a few hundred yards for Clint to see tracks coming out of the water. The outlaws had left hoof prints in the mud from the stream, but then the tracks faded away. Clint dismounted, walked around a bit and finally found what he was looking for. He fired a shot to signal Crown and waited.

***

Sheriff Crown heard the shot, turned his horse and rode back up the creek. By the time he arrived, Clint Adams had dismounted and was down on one knee.

"There," he said, pointing.

Crown looked, squinting.

"Are you sure?"

Clint stood up.

"Those are definite brush marks," he said. "Somebody brushed away their tracks. Notice how the ground gets harder up ahead?"

"No tracks there," Crown said.

Clint mounted up and looked at his friend.

"We just have to keep going," he said. "We'll find their trail again."

"I'm gonna trust you, Clint," Crown said. "Like I said before, it's been a while for me."

"You won't be sorry, Ed," Clint assured him.

"I hope not," Crown said. "I told you my butt was getting' used to bein' in the saddle again, but I can't say the same for my back."

Chapter Twenty-Eight

Although Cornville was a small town, it had everything it needed to survive, including shops, saloons and hotels.

Manning and Bailey rode in at dusk, with Linda asleep in front of her father.

"This is it?" Bailey asked.

"This is it," Manning said. "If they catch up to us, we'll make a stand here."

"Against Adams?"

"I just need to put together enough guns," Manning said.

Bailey looked around at the quiet street.

"Does it get livelier than this?" he asked.

"Don't worry," Manning said, "you'll find enough to entertain you while I take care of business."

"What about the woman you said you had here?"

"She's part of the business," Manning said. "Her name's Molly Tanner, and she owns a couple of saloons in town." What Manning didn't tell Bailey was that he was not only sleeping with Molly Tanner, but he worked for her.

"In fact, this is one of hers." Manning reined in his horse in front of a saloon called MOLLY'S CORNER. There were lights and piano music coming from inside. "I'm gonna go in and tell 'er we're here."

"Then what?"

"Then we'll go to the hotel and get settled," Manning said.

"What about the kid?"

Manning took his sleeping daughter off his horse and walked over to Bailey. He handed the girl up to him.

"Just hang onto her and let 'er sleep."

"I tol' you I ain't no babysitter."

"I know you ain't," Manning said. "This'll be the last time you even have to see her."

Bailey looked down at the sleeping child in his arms.

"Yeah, okay," he said. "How long you gonna be?"

"That depends," Manning said and went into the saloon. He didn't tell Bailey that it depended on whether or not Molly would want to fuck as soon as she saw him.

***

As Clint had predicted, they picked up the trail again, but he could tell they had lost a few hours on them.

"We're half a day behind them, now," he said, mounting up after examining the ground.

"Shit," Crown complained.

"It's getting dark," Clint said. "We'll have to camp and start picking up ground again in the morning."

"If they're smart enough to throw us off the scent once, they can do it again," Crown complained.

"We won't let them," Clint said, "because we know they're smart enough to try it."

They made camp and Clint prepared their supper of beans and coffee.

"You figure they're just runnin'?" Crown asked. "Or are they headin' somewhere in particular?"

"The way they had everything planned," Clint said, "I bet they're heading someplace in particular."

"I hope you're right," Crown said. "Maybe if they get there and stop a while, we'll finally catch up."

"We're going to catch them, Ed," Clint said, "and get that little girl back to her mother."

"And the money back to the bank."

"Yeah, that, too," Clint said. He knew the money was Crown's main concern because he was the law, but he was worried about the little girl. A recent encounter with a small boy at Christmas time seemed to make Clint more sympathetic to what the little girl and her mother were going through.

"I'll take first watch," Crown said, "just in case. I ain't ready to go to sleep anyway."

"Fine with me," Clint said. "Wake me in about four hours."

***

The bartender knew Manning. Although he hadn't seen him in some weeks, he waved him on through. Manning went to the back and knocked on a door.

"Come!" a woman's voice called.

He opened the door and went in. Molly Tanner looked up from her desk, saw him and smiled. She was wearing one of her dresses that caused her big breasts to look as if they were going to spill out at any minute. She knew her customers liked it.

"Well, whataya know?" she said. "He's back."

"I told you I'd come back."

"Hey," she said, "for all I knew you were gonna take one look at that ex-wife of yours and stay away."

"Not a chance, Molly," he said, taking off his hat and tossing it aside. "You know you're the only woman for me."

"I better be," she said, standing up.

At forty she was still a fine figure of a woman, with a smooth, unlined face and shoulders to match. Her dark hair, slightly streaked with grey, was piled high on her head.

"You got the money?" she asked, approaching him.

"Yeah, Bailey's got it on his horse, just outside," Manning said. "He's waitin' for me to come out."

Molly got right up close to him, then peeled the dress down from her shoulders so that those big breasts tumbled out at him.

"Let 'im wait," she said.

Chapter Twenty-Nine

Manning took her into his arms and kissed her, at the same time peeling the dress off the rest of the way. Then he lifted the naked woman off her feet and set her down on her big desk. Paper and books went flying to the floor as he undid his trousers, freed his hard cock and drove it into her. This was going to be quick, but he knew later they would spend more time together.

"Ain't had it since I been gone, huh?" he asked.

"You know I keep it for you when you're away," she told him.

As he drove himself in and out of her, he leaned over to devour her big, brown nipples. She raked his back with her nails as she implored him to fuck her harder, faster. They grunted and groaned with the effort, although they were both careful not to be heard from the saloon.

When he exploded inside of her, they both bit their lip to keep from shouting, and then he backed up and pulled up his pants.

"That'll do for now," she said, breathlessly, as she climbed back into her dress. "We don't want Mr. Bailey getting impatient and lighting out with the money."

"He knows better," Manning said. "Besides, he's got Linda."

"Linda?" She walked back around her desk while he picked up the papers and things that had been swept off.

"My daughter," he said. "I tol' you I was gonna be seein' her."

"Yes, but you didn't tell me you'd be bringing her back with you."

"Well . . . I didn't know I was."

"What do you plan to do with her?" she asked.

"I dunno," he said. "I'll have to get somebody to watch her for a while."

"Don't look at me," she said. "I'm not a babysitter, and a saloon is no place for a child."

"Don't worry," he said. "I wasn't gonna saddle you with her."

"You're damn right you weren't," she said. "How did everything go at the bank?"

"Fine," he said, "except . . . some people got killed."

"You can't make eggs without breaking the shells," she said. "How many?"

"Three."

"That many? Not good. What about the old lawman?"

"He's on our trail."

She frowned.

"We didn't expect that," she said. "You told me he was sixty if he was a day."

"He is, but . . . he got some help."

"A posse?" she said. "You also told me he wouldn't be able to get up a posse."

"Uh, no, not a posse." He sat in the chair in front of her desk.

"Then who?"

"Um, one man."

She glared at him.

"Are you going to make me guess?"

"Clint Adams."

Her fine eyebrows went up.

"The Gunsmith? What the hell was he doing there?"

"I don't know," Manning said, "but there he was, and he and the lawman are on our trail."

"Are you sure?"

"I sent Lyle Victor to check our back trail . . ."

"And?"

". . . and we ain't seen 'im since."

"So you think he ran into them and got caught?"

"Or killed."

"Damn it," she said, sitting back in her chair. "You told me that bank would be easy."

"It was," Manning said, then added, "well, it shoulda been."

"Who got killed?"

"The bank manager, a teller and a citizen out on the street who tried to play hero."

"And who's fault was that?"

"Bailey got trigger happy," Manning lied. "And Lyle panicked."

"You told me they were good boys," Molly said. "Am I not gonna be able to trust you, Des?"

"You know you can trust me, Molly," he said. "I just have to make sure I get better boys."

"Right."

"And fast," he said.

"How far behind you do you think Adams and the old lawman are?"

"I'm thinkin' half a day."

"Then you better get busy collecting some guns to back you up."

"And the money?"

"I told you," he said. "Bailey's got it."

"Well," she said, "you had better get it away from him, hadn't you?"

"Right," he said, standing.

Chapter Thirty

Clint woke Sheriff Crown the following morning with a cup of coffee.

"I thought we'd just have coffee and get an early start," he said.

"Sounds like a good idea to me," Crown said.

They finished their coffee, doused the fire and saddled their horses.

"You know," Clint said, as they started riding, "if they decide to split up, we'll have to do the same. Are you prepared for that?"

"I have to be, don't I?" Crown answered. "But let's deal with that if and when it happens."

"Deal," Clint said.

***

The night before, after leaving Molly's Corner, Manning had Bailey take care of the horses while he got a room in the hotel so he could get Linda into a bed for the night. Then he could go to Molly's room and give her a proper hello.

"Then get a room for yourself and stash the money under the bed."

"You really trust me with all this money?" Bailey asked.

"If you take it and run, I'll find you, Bailey," Manning said. "You know that."

Bailey looked away.

"Yeah, I do."

***

Manning woke the next morning with Linda sitting beside him, staring.

"Why are you lookin' at me?" he asked.

"I was waiting for you to wake up, Pa," she said. "I'm hungry."

"What time is it?" he demanded, looking around.

"I don't know," she said. "I'm hungry."

"Right, right," he said, rubbing his face with his hand. "Okay, we'll get dressed and go and get some breakfast."

"I *am* dressed," she said.

And she was, of course, in the same clothes she'd had on when they left Willow Springs.

"And I'm stinky," she said, "like you."

"You need a bath," he said.

"So do you."

"First things first," he said. "We'll eat, then find something clean for you to wear. And then you'll have your bath."

"And you, too?"

"Don't get smart," he growled.

"I am smart," she said. "Mama says so."

"Never mind what your Mama says," Manning said. "Just be quiet while I get dressed."

Linda folded her arms and sulked.

***

Bailey Wilkins sat in his room with the money bags on the bed. He had been thinking about two things ever since he woke up and got dressed. First, getting breakfast and two, lighting out with the money and taking the chance that Manning would never find him. After all, forty thousand dollars was forty thousand dollars.

He didn't even know why a small bank in a town like Willow Springs would have forty thousand dollars in their safe, but somehow Manning had found out. A three-way split of that much money was a decent take. Now that Lyle Victor had disappeared, the split was an even nicer fifty-fifty. But taking it all would be a windfall like he had never seen before. The only thing he had to decide was, did he want to be looking over his shoulder for the rest of his life?

***

Molly Tanner woke the next morning feeling pleasantly sore. Manning had come to her room that night and they had fucked until they were both out of breath. Then he went back to his own room because he had "his little girl."

Now, as Molly dressed, she wondered if the little one was going to be a problem? She also wondered if Bailey Wilkins was going to be a problem? She didn't like the fact that Manning was leaving the money in Bailey's possession. She had a good mind to send one of her "side guns"—gunmen she used for small side jobs—to get the money and kill him. But, in the end, she decided to trust Manning that Bailey would not run off with the whole thing.

She could keep a couple of her side guns ready, though. Just in case. Who knew? She might even have to get rid of both men. But it would take two men to replace Manning. One to plan the jobs, and one to see to her personal needs. So far Manning had been competent at both tasks. It remained to be seen if this job—and the little girl—were going to be the breaking point in their relationship.

Chapter Thirty-One

"There," Clint said, pointing.

"You know," Crown said, "when I read, I need these damned spectacles." He patted his shirt pocket. "Maybe I should be wearin' them for this job, too."

"Don't worry about it, Ed," Clint said. "I can see well enough for both of us."

They followed the trail for most of the day, stopped a few times to rest the horses.

"It don't seem like they stop as much as we do to rest," Crown said. "Not even with a little girl."

"What's it matter?" Clint asked. "She's not walking. She's probably asleep most of the time, anyway. I don't think she'll slow them down all that much."

"I'm kinda surprised he's kept her this long," Crown said. "If he was tryin' to hurt her mother, why didn't he just dump her somewhere along the way—I mean, at some ranch or homestead."

"Maybe being a father means more to him than he thought it would," Clint said.

"Somehow," Crown said, "that doesn't sound like a man who would take children hostage, rob a bank and commit murder."

"Then we really need to get to that kid fast," Clint said.

***

When Manning walked into the hotel dining room with Linda, he saw Bailey sitting at a table. At his feet were two drawstring sacks.

Manning put Linda in one seat and took the other, right across from Bailey.

"I assume these sacks are the money," he said, in a low voice.

"I didn't think it would look good for me to be sittin' here with two bank bags at my feet."

"Pa, can I have flapjacks?"

"Sure, why not?" Manning said.

When the waiter came over, he ordered flapjacks for both of them. Bailey continued to eat his eggs.

"Molly wants the money today," he told Bailey.

"Why?"

"She wants to count it."

"Again, why?" Bailey asked. "How's she involved?"

"Look," Manning said, "Molly bankrolled the job. She's bankrolled a lot of my jobs, so she gets a cut."

"So it was never a three-way cut, it was a four-way?"

"She don't get an even share," Manning said. "But she does the count."

Bailey frowned.

"I don't think I like your woman gettin' all the money," he said.

"Don't worry," Manning said, "we can stand there while she counts it."

"I still don't like it."

"Look, you've kept the money safe all this time," Manning said. "Don't worry, you're gonna get your cut, and your share of Lyle's cut."

"I better."

The waiter brought the flapjacks and put them down in front of his customers, together with a dish of butter and a pitcher of syrup.

"I don't want butter, but I want lots of syrup!" Linda exclaimed, happily.

Manning picked up the pitcher and poured a generous dollop onto her plate.

"More, Pa, more!" she yelled.

"You eat that and then I'll pour more," he told her, adding some to his own plate. He looked at Bailey. "After breakfast we'll go and see Molly."

"What about the kid?" Bailey asked.

Manning looked at Linda, who was happily stuffing her face with flapjacks.

"We'll take her with us."

"How's your woman gonna like that?" Bailey asked.

"I guess we'll find out."

***

The saloon doors were locked when they got there, so Manning pounded his fist on it.

"Pa, I thought I was gonna get a new dress," Linda said.

"You are," he said, "later, after your bath."

"I'm stinky," she said to Bailey. "Like you."

Bailey ignored her.

The door was opened by the bartender, whose name was Emmett. He was a stocky man in his fifties, with a great head of black hair.

"Boss around, Emmett?" Manning asked.

"In the office. Go on back." He looked down. "Who's this little urchin?"

"That's my daughter, Linda."

Emmett stared at the kid as they entered the saloon.

"You know the boss don't like kids," he said. "I wouldn't take her back there if I was you."

"I don't have any place to leave 'er," Manning said.

"Leave her with me."

"With you?" Manning said. "A bartender?"

"I'm also a father and a grandfather," Emmett said. "Believe me, I know how to handle kids."

"Are you serious?"

"Come on, little one," Emmett said, lifting Linda off the floor. "Come and sit on the bar."

"Wheeeee!" Linda squealed.

"Well, okay, then," Manning said. "Come, Bailey, let's get this over with."

Together, they walked to the back and knocked on the office door.

***

"How do you like bein' with your Pa, little one?" Emmett asked, as Linda sat on the bar and swung her legs.

"I don't," she said. "My butt hurts from bein' on a horse, and I smell like a horse."

"You need a bath."

"Pa was supposed ta gimme one this mornin'," she said. "And buy me a new dress."

"Well," Emmett said, "maybe you and me can do somethin' about that."

Chapter Thirty-Two

Molly looked up from her desk as the two men entered her office.

"I don't know why I expected you to have your kid with you," she said to Manning.

"I did," he said. "She's out there with Emmett. Apparently, he likes kids."

Molly looked at Bailey.

"Oh, Molly Tanner, this is Bailey Wilkins," Manning said. "Bailey, give Molly the cash."

Bailey hesitated.

"Bailey—" Manning said.

"I'm still not sure about this," Bailey said.

Molly looked at Manning.

Manning looked at Bailey.

"What the hell—" he said, but he was interrupted by a shot.

Molly had reached into her top drawer and come out with a gun. Bailey, unfortunately for him, was holding the cash bags in his right hand—his gun hand. His eyes widened and he dropped the bags so he could grab for his gun, but he was too late. Molly shot him, hitting him in the chest. He dropped to the floor, dead.

She turned the gun on Manning.

"Am I going to have trouble with you, too?"

"Not me," Manning said, bending over and picking up the money bags. He carried them to the desk and set them down in front of her.

"It doesn't upset you that I killed him?"

"He was askin' for it," Manning said. "I kept waitin' for him to make a break with the money. Then I would've killed him myself."

She nodded, satisfied, and put the gun back in the drawer. Then she opened both sacks and dumped the cash onto her desk.

"Forty thousand?" she said.

"That's what it's supposed to be."

"Sit down and watch me count it."

He sat and watched as she started counting the money.

"Well?" he asked, when she was finished.

"Forty-two thousand," she said. "That's eighty-four hundred for me." She stared at him. "You're making out pretty well, not having to split with your two men."

"It's not my fault they managed to get themselves killed," he said.

"I'll put the money in my safe," she said.

"I'll take my cut now," he said.

"And do what? Put it in your room? If word got out, you wouldn't last long. Don't worry, it'll be safe here with me. You can have it when you decide to leave." She put the money back in the bags, and the bags in the safe behind her. Then she looked at him. "That is, if you decide to leave."

"I can think of a reason or two to stay," he said. "But I've also got trouble on my trail—trouble named the Gunsmith."

"Don't worry about him," she said. "I can give you as many guns as you want to back your play."

"I'll take those guns. Then it looks like me and my daughter'll be stayin' around for a while."

"Is that gonna be a problem?" he asked.

"Not as long as you keep her away far from me," Molly said, holding both hands up.

"Don't worry," he said. "The things I wanna do with you won't concern her, at all. Besides, I might not be keepin' her all that much longer."

"Why's that?"

"She's startin' to become too demandin'," Manning said. "Like a woman. Speakin' of which, she needs a bath and some new clothes."

"Go take care of her, then," Molly said. "I'll see you back here later. I should have some men for you, by then."

"What about him?" Manning asked, pointing to Bailey's body.

"Don't worry," she said. "I'll take care of him.

***

Outside in the saloon, Manning found Linda sitting on the bar, laughing with Emmett.

"This girl needs a bath," the bartender said. "And some clean clothes."

"I know it. I guess I could just take 'er over to the barber shop."

"Hell, no," Emmett said. "We ain't openin' for a while. If it's okay with you, I'll take her home with me and my wife can give her a bath."

"What about some clothes?"

"We've still got some of our granddaughter's clothes when she was this small."

"That sounds good to me," Manning said.

"Just leave 'er with me and my misses for a while," Emmett said. "We'll take care of 'er."

"That suits me," Manning said. "She's gettin' to be a pain, anyway. Linda, you go with Emmett."

"Okay, Pa," she said. "I like 'im."

"That's good," Manning said, and left.

Chapter Thirty-Three

"They keep bypassing the larger towns," Clint said. "So they must be heading for some town in particular."

"But which one?" Crown asked. "There are any number of small towns ahead."

"As long as I can keep picking up their trail, they'll lead us to it," Clint said.

"There's three towns up ahead," Crown said. "Barton, Gault and Cornville. They could be headin' for one of those."

"Or beyond," Clint said.

Crown rubbed his lower back and said, "I hope not. I don't know how much longer I can do this."

"They're either going to think they shook us, or set a trap for us," Clint said. "Either way, we'll find them."

***

Manning was happy to get the little girl off his hands. He had other plans to make. If Molly was going to give him some men to help him handle Clint Adams and the lawman from Willow Springs, then he had some purchases to make. If he was going to face the Gunsmith, he wanted to be properly outfitted.

He left the saloon and headed for the mercantile store, and then the gun shop.

***

Molly looked up as her door opened again. The man who came in almost tripped over Bailey's body.

"That's one reason I sent for you, Crabbe," she said. "I need you to dispose of that body."

"No problem," Buck Crabbe said. "I'll have a couple of my boys do it. What's Emmett doin' with that little girl?"

"He had her with him when he found you?"

"Yeah, said he was takin' her home."

"She belongs to Des Manning. She's his daughter, but he doesn't really want her."

"Cute kid."

"You want her?"

"Hell, no," Crabbe said. "What would I do with a kid?"

Crabbe, at thirty, was about ten years younger than Molly, but that didn't stop her from taking him to bed when Manning wasn't around.

"What's Manning doin' back here?" he asked.

"He did a job, and came back with the money," she said. "Now he's got some trouble trailing him."

"A posse?"

She shook her head.

"One lawman . . . and Clint Adams."

Crabbe's eye widened.

"The Gunsmith? He's gonna track 'im here?"

"It's likely," she said. "That's the other job I have for you."

"Kill the Gunsmith?" Crabbe asked. "I can do that."

"I want you to back Manning's play, whatever it is," she said. "So it may come to killing the Gunsmith, but let him call it."

"Am I comin' to your room tonight?" he asked.

"No, not tonight."

"Is that why I didn't come last night?" Crabbe asked. "Because you were with him?"

"Never mind," Molly said. "I'll let you know when I need you between my legs. Right now, I need you for these other two jobs."

Crabbe looked down at the dead man.

"Who killed him?"

"I did," she said.

"All right. I'll have two of my boys come in and get rid of him. Then I'll find Manning."

"Good," she said. "Come back sometime tonight and let me know how it went with him."

"I'll be back," he said. "Count on it."

Chapter Thirty-Four

Manning made the purchases he thought he needed to deal with Clint Adams. Then went back to Molly's, now that it was open for business. Emmett was behind the bar when he ordered a beer.

"Your girl's with my wife," the bartender said, not that Linda's father had asked about her.

"Huh? Oh, good, good."

Manning walked away from the bar and sat at a table. Moments later a man came through the batwing doors, looked around, and joined him.

"What do you want?" Manning asked.

"The name's Crabbe," the other man said. "Molly said you might need some backup against the Gunsmith."

"Oh yeah," Manning said. "Get yerself a beer and let's talk."

Crabbe went to the bar, came back with a beer and sat down.

"She said she had guns for me," Manning said. "How many men you got?"

"Six behind me, unless you think you need more," Crabbe said.

"Eight men against the Gunsmith and an old law-man? I think that might do it."

"Who's this old lawman?"

"Don't know his name," Manning said. "Just know he's sixty if he's a day."

To thirty-year-old Crabbe, that sounded ancient.

"I guess eight guns should do it, then," he agreed.

"What I'd really like to do," Crabbe said, "is try him by myself first."

"Are you serious?" Manning asked. "Are you that good?"

"Don't you find that out by goin' up against the best?" Crabbe asked.

"You could also get killed."

"Yeah, but people would remember me."

Manning stared at Crabbe for a few moments.

"All right," he said, then, "when he gets here, why don't we see if he's willin'? And I can take care of the lawman. Your other guns can back our play, if it comes to that."

"I can have 'em here in an hour, if you wanna meet them tonight."

"I do," Manning said. "There's no tellin' when Ad-ams is gonna get here."

Crabbe downed his beer, stood up and said, "I'll be back."

"I'll be here," Manning said, and watched the younger man go out the door, wondering if he was any good with a handgun, at all?

When he turned his head to check the action in the saloon, he saw Molly walking toward him. She was wearing a mint green gown with her trademark plunging neckline. Men were watching her hungrily as she walked.

She sat across from him and waved one of the young saloon girls over.

"Yes, Miss Tanner?"

"Bring me a glass of champagne, Darlene."

"Yes, Ma'am."

She folded her hands on top of the table and stared at Manning.

"Was that Crabbe I saw leaving here?"

"That was him," Manning said. "Real good one you picked to back my play."

"What do you mean?"

"He wants to try Adams on his own."

She gave the matter some thought.

"He might be that good," she admitted.

"Are you serious?"

"Deadly."

Darlene came over and put down a glass of champagne.

"The good stuff, Ma'am," she said. "Your private stock."

"Thank you, Darlene."

The girl went back to work in the rapidly filling saloon.

"He's likely to get himself killed tryin' to make a name for himself," Manning said.

"What do you care if he kills Adams or gets killed?" she asked. "You'll be there to pick up the pieces."

He grinned at her.

"Molly," he said, "that must be why we get along. We're so much alike."

"We get along because you know your place, Des," she said. "And tonight, your place is in my bed. Can you leave your kid with Emmett and his wife?"

"I'm sure Emmett's wife would love that," he said. "What time?"

"Midnight," she said, sipping her champagne, "I'll be ready for you at midnight. That is, providing Clint Adams doesn't arrive between now and then."

"It's gettin' dark and I'm sure he won't wanna ride in at night," he said.

She finished her champagne and set the empty glass down.

"What are you doing now?" she asked.

"Waitin' for your man, Crabbe," he said. "He's comin' back to introduce me to his men."

"Pity," she said, standing up. "We could have had a quick poke in my office."

As she walked away, he opened his mouth to call her back, but decided against it. Midnight would be soon enough.

Chapter Thirty-Five

When Buck Crabbe returned, he had six men with him. All but one seemed to be around thirty, like he was. The last one looked to be about fifty, probably the only one with any seasoning. He left them at the bar and joined Manning, again.

"That's them?" Manning asked.

"Yep."

"Only one looks like he knows one end of his gun from the other."

"That's Benson," Crabbe said. "He's good. Almost as good as me."

"And the others?"

"They can shoot. Wanna meet 'em one-by-one or all together?"

"I wanna meet Benson," Manning said. "I have the feelin' he'll be able to tell me all I need to know."

"I'll bring 'im over."

"Along with two beers," Manning said.

"Nothin' for him?" Crabbe asked, as he stood.

"Nothing for you."

***

When Benson walked over carrying two beers, Crabbe remained at the bar with the other five men. From the looks of things, they were talking about Manning.

"Thanks for the beer," Benson said, sitting down. He placed both glasses in front of himself.

"Yeah," Manning said, reaching out and grabbing a glass, "one's for me."

"Oh, sure. Crabbe says you got some questions about me."

"Not about you," Manning said. "I think I got you figured just by lookin' at you."

"That so?"

"I wanna talk about them," Manning said, jerking his chin toward the other men.

"I don't know 'em," Benson said.

"What about Crabbe?"

"Him I know," Benson said. "I do jobs for him sometimes."

"Why?"

"He pays me."

"How?"

"Molly pays him."

"That I get," Manning said.

"You work for her?" Benson asked, after a sip of beer.

"We work together," Manning said.

"Uh-huh," Benson said. "You gonna be usin' them others?"

"That's what Crabbe says," Manning answered. "Did he tell you what the job is?"

"Backin' your play against the law. I'm all for that."

"It's not just the law," Manning said. "It's Clint Adams."

"The Gunsmith is comin' here?" Benson asked, shocked.

"And Crabbe wants a shot at him, alone."

"Then he's a dead man walkin'," Benson said.

"I was told he's good with a gun."

"Who told you that?"

"Molly. And Crabbe."

"What'd he say?"

"He said you were almost as good as he was," Manning said. "I'm thinkin' he's stretchin' the truth."

"A lot," Benson said. "On his best day . . ." Benson stopped and shook his head.

"So," Manning said, "you're willin' to back me with them backin' you?"

"Hey," Benson said, "it's a job. If I was you, though, I'd talk to each one, make your own decision."

"I was hopin' you'd help me do that," Manning said, "but . . . yeah, sure, send the first one over."

***

He took the men one-by-one, but they were pretty much all the same. More bravado than brains.

Crabbe had apparently left it to Manning to tell them about Clint Adams. Four of them got excited, while two looked pretty nervous. But they were all willing to do the job.

When he finished with the last one Crabbe came back over, carrying two beers.

"Thanks," Manning said.

"So whataya think?" Crabbe asked.

"I think I can use Benson," Manning said. "Maybe you. The others . . ."

"You might just need them to stand there behind you," Crabbe said. "You know, a show of force. Maybe the lawman and Adams will turn and run."

"Not likely," Manning said. "I've never heard anythin' about the Gunsmith runnin' from a fight. And the lawman is an old-timer. He won't run."

"Then you'll need all the guns you can get," Crabbe said, looking over at the men at the bar. "They may not be fast, but they'll shoot."

Manning nodded.

"I guess that's what counts."

Chapter Thirty-Six

Clint and Crown noticed that the tracks they were following were not only bypassing large towns, but the small ones, as well.

"What about Cornville, up ahead?" Crown asked. "Should we just keep goin'?" The tracks had faded once again.

"Let's wait til we get closer to decide," Clint said. "We might pick the trail up again. Do you know anything about the town?"

"Not a thing," Crown said. "I haven't been up this far north of Lincoln."

"The horses could use a little rest," Clint said, thinking more of Crown's horse, as well as the man's backside.

"Tell me about it," Crown said. "My back's killin' me. But we don't wanna fall further behind, again."

Days in the saddle were taking a toll on the older lawman. He was starting to look haggard and worn. On the other hand, Clint was very pleased with the performance of his Tobiano. Toby didn't seem to be the slightest out of breath, even when they stopped at night.

"Let's take a break," Clint said, dismounting.

"Not on my account," Crown said, but he also dismounted and stretched, rubbing his lower back.

Clint stood in front of Toby and rubbed his nose. But he was looking past the horse at Crown, thinking the man seemed older than he had ever before.

"You going to be all right?" he asked.

"I'm fine," Crown said. "Come on, let's get goin'. I wanna catch up."

They both mounted up and Clint started studying the ground again as they rode, trying to pick up the trail.

***

"There it is!"

Crown rode up alongside Clint.

"Are you sure?"

Clint pointed.

"I don't even have to dismount," Clint said. "That's them. Now let's see where they take us."

They followed the tracks for a couple of hours, and then Clint reined in again.

"Now what?"

"Cornville," Clint said. "That's where they're headed."

"Are you sure?"

"We saw that sign a few miles back," Clint said. "Cornville's five miles ahead. These tracks are heading right in that direction."

"Then I guess we're goin' to Cornville," Crown said.

"I guess we are."

***

Manning rolled over in bed and bumped into a naked Molly Tanner.

"Is that your subtle way of wakin' me up?" she asked, her head buried in her pillow.

"Sorry," he said. "I'm not used to sleepin' with somebody else."

She picked up her head and looked at him.

"Why *are* you here?" she asked. "You never spent the night before. You always give me a good poke, and then you're on your way."

"I guess I was pretty tired," he said. "I just . . . fell asleep."

He tossed back the sheet and swung his feet to the floor.

"Now you're leaving?" she said.

"I gotta get ready."

"For the Gunsmith?"

"For whatever comes," he said, pulling on his trousers.

"Did Crabbe come up with some men?" she asked.

"I think he came up with one," Manning said. "There are a few others, but only one I can probably count on."

She sat up in bed, holding the sheet up to cover her nudity.

"I told him to get you some good men to back you," she said. "If he doesn't, I'll—"

"Don't worry about it," Manning said, buttoning his shirt. "I can take care of it."

"You sure?" she asked.

"Positive."

She laid back down, the sheet molding itself to her full body.

"Sure you want to leave?" she asked, stretching.

"No," he said, "but I better."

She sat up again as he headed for the door.

"When this is all over," she said, "and you've killed the Gunsmith, are you going to be too big a man to work with me anymore?"

He paused, as if thinking it over.

"Huh," he finally replied, "you never know."

Chapter Thirty-Seven

Manning met with Buck Crabbe that morning for breakfast. They agreed that one of Crabbe's men would be on watch for a stranger riding from that point forward.

"They may not know what the Gunsmith looks like," Manning said, "but I just want to know when any stranger rides into town."

"Right."

"And I want Benson available at all times," Manning ordered.

"I'll make sure," Crabbe promised.

"And this is important," Manning added. "Nobody is to approach them. I'm gonna want to make sure they're Adams and the lawman before we do anythin'. You got that?"

"Got it."

"This is for you, too, Crabbe," Manning said. "If you think it's the Gunsmith, don't try to face him yourself."

Crabbe hesitated.

"Like I said," Manning went on. "Let's make sure who they are before we do *anything*."

"I get it, Manning," Crabbe said.

"Make sure you do," Manning said. "I don't want them warned before we're ready to take 'em."

"I understood you pulled a job for Molly," Crabbe said. "Where are your partners from that one?"

"Gone," was all Manning would say. "Don't worry about them."

***

After breakfast, Crabbe went to instruct his men, while Manning went back to his hotel room. He had bought himself a new shotgun and a good selection of shells. He decided to clean the gun to make sure it would work when the time came. He knew he would be no match for Clint Adams with a handgun, but the scattergun might give him an edge. The buckshot shells he bought would scatter and spread, making it hard for him to miss.

But just to be on the safe side, he also bought a brand new holster, one that he thought would enable him to draw his Colt faster.

While cleaning the shotgun, though, he had another thought. Molly didn't know it, but he had once watched very closely as she opened her safe, which meant he knew the combination. Why didn't he just let Crabbe, Benson and the others handle Adams and the lawman, while he took the forty thousand from the safe and left town? Even if the Gunsmith and the lawman somehow came out on top, it would be a while before they got on his trail, again. Of course, that would mean ending his partnership—and relationship—with Molly Tanner.

A move like that would take some more thought . . .

***

Crabbe also had some thinking to do.

He had been warned about facing the Gunsmith by himself, without the others, but that was actually what he wanted to do. If he was successful, and killed Clint Adams, what did he care what Des Manning would say? And it mattered even less if Adams managed to kill him.

This was supposed to be a job that Molly was paying him to do. But once he heard the Gunsmith was involved, he started thinking about making a name for himself, and then leaving Cornville. What a terrible name for a town. He didn't know why they never changed it. But then he wasn't a politician, just a gunman for hire. And he wanted to be more than that.

He wanted to be a known gun.

***

Molly opened her safe, sat back and stared at the money there. The forty thousand Manning had brought back from Willow Springs made the total ninety thousand. It had always been her plan to make a hundred thousand dollars, and then get out of Cornville and move on. If it wasn't for the fact that most of the forty was supposed to be Manning's, she would almost be at her goal. In fact, she could settle for the ninety now and be on her way before anyone knew she was gone.

She took a bottle from her bottom desk drawer, poured herself a drink and continued to stare.

***

Clint reined in and pointed ahead.

"There it is," he said, "and the tracks lead right into town."

"Cornville," Crown said. "I wonder if they're still there."

"If they are," Clint said, "which one of us would they recognize, riding in?"

Crown scratched the stubble on his jaw.

"Well, you're the Gunsmith," he said.

"You're the law."

"I am in Willow Springs," Crown reminded him. "Not so much here." He took the badge off his shirt and put it in his pocket, as he had already done a few times during this hunt.

"Why don't I just ride on in and have a look around," Crown said. "You can wait out here."

"You're not going to recognize any of them, either," Clint said.

"Neither are you," Crown said. "I'll just ride in, have a drink, and see if any strangers have ridden into town. If so, I'll see if they're still around. If they are, I'll come back and get ya."

"Don't try to take them alone, Ed," Clint warned.

"I won't," Crown said, "believe me. I may be the law, but I'm no hero."

Chapter Thirty-Eight

It was getting on toward dusk when Sheriff Ed Crown rode into Cornville, hoping he just looked like some old timer.

There were several saloons, even though Cornville wasn't that large of a town. He decided to simply choose the biggest one, so he stopped in front of the well-lit and loud Golden Ace Saloon and went inside.

He was a stranger, so he expected to attract a little attention, but not as much if he had walked in with his badge on.

The bartender came over and asked, "What can I getcha, old timer?" which was encouraging.

"Beer."

"Sure thing."

The bartender set a glass of beer on the bar. Crown drank half of it down, gratefully.

"Oh, yeah," he said, setting the glass down. "That's what I needed. Nice and cold."

"The only way beer should be," the bartender said. "Just ride in?"

"Almost to the minute," Crown said. "I'm hopin' you don't get so many strangers I won't be able to find a room."

"Not many strangers in town, at all," the bartender said. "You should be able to get a room easy. Try the Fletcher Hotel, on the corner."

"I'll do that," Crown said, "as soon as I finish my beer.

***

Benson walked into Molly's, saw Manning sitting alone at a table and walked over.

"One stranger just rode in," he said.

"You think it's Adams?"

"Not unless Clint Adams is in his sixties."

"The old sheriff," Manning said. "He came in alone?"

Benson nodded.

"All by his lonesome."

"Where is he?"

"He went into the Golden Ace."

"Where's Crabbe?"

"He went over there to take a look at 'im," Benson said. "Would you know 'im from Willow Springs if you saw 'im?"

"Oh yeah," Manning said. "I looked 'im over before I did the job. We better get over there so I can have a look."

Manning stood and the two men headed for the door.

"Where are Crabbe's other men?" Manning asked.

"Around town," Benson said. "A couple might even already be in the Golden Ace."

"Let's hope nobody does nothin' stupid," Manning said.

"This town ain't had a lawman in a long time," Benson said. "People are doin' stupid shit every day."

***

When Crabbe entered the Golden Ace, he saw the old timer who had just ridden in, standing at the bar. He had sent Benson to tell Manning, but he wanted a look at the stranger, himself. He doubted it was The Gunsmith, but maybe he could send Clint Adams a message.

Crabbe looked around, saw two of his men sitting at a table with beers in front of them. He pointed to the bar, but then waved at them to stay seated, just watch and be ready.

He walked to the bar and stood a few feet down from the stranger. He heard him talking to the bartender about a hotel. When the old man turned to leave, Crabbe barred his way.

"'scuse me," the man said.

Crabbe looked him over closely.

"Sorry," he said. "Didn't mean to get in your way."

"That's all right, son," the older man said.

As he started to turn away Crabbe asked, loudly, "Those holes in your shirt mean anythin'?"

"What's that?" Crown frowned.

"Holes," Crabbe said, touching his shirt, "where a badge would be."

Crown looked down at his shirt, saw all the holes where he had pinned on and taken off his badge many times. This fella was observant.

"That was the ol' days, friend," he said. "A long while back, but I still got all the shirts."

"So you ain't a lawman anymore," Crabbe said.

"Not for a long time. You mind if I go, now? I gotta turn in. I been on the trail a while, and at my age I need all the rest I can get."

"Sure thing, ol' timer," Crabbe said, "sure thing. Go ahead."

Sheriff Crown nodded, turned and went through the batwing doors.

***

"Stop!" Manning said to Benson.

"What is it?" Benson asked.

"That's him," Manning said. "That's the sheriff from Willow Springs. His name's Crown."

"Then where's the Gunsmith?" Benson wondered. "Still inside?"

"We'll have to wait and see," Manning said.

As they watched, however, Buck Crabbe came through the doors and watched as the old lawman mounted his horse and turned it.

"Hey, old timer!" Crabbe shouted. "The hotel's the other way."

As they watched, Manning knew Crabbe was about to do something stupid.

The lawman turned to face Crabbe.

"Why don't you take the badge outta your pocket and pin it on," Crabbe said. "You ain't foolin' anybody. You were pretty interested in strangers comin' to town."

"And what's your interest?" Crown asked.

"I live here," he said. "I don't like lawmen comin' to town, even if they're ex-lawmen. But I don't think that's the case with you."

"What if that's true?" Crown asked.

"Then pin on your badge and go for your gun," Crabbe told him.

"What's he doin'?" Benson said.

"Bein' a fool," Manning said.

But they stood there and watched, without intervening.

Chapter Thirty-Nine

Crown's intention was to ride to another saloon and see what he could find out there, but as he turned his horse, the fellow who had blocked him came out the doors of the saloon and shouted at him.

"Why would I go for my gun?" Crown asked. "I got nothin' against you."

"Well, I got somethin' against you," the man said. "I could see the outline of that damn badge in your pocket."

Crown looked down, figured he had no choice, took the badge out and pinned it on.

"Where's your friend, the Gunsmith, now?" the gunman asked.

"Don't you worry," Crown said. "You'll be seein' him soon."

"Yeah, well soon you won't be seein' nothin'."

He drew his gun.

***

While Manning and Benson watched, Crabbe drew his gun quickly and fired. The bullet knocked the law-man off his horse. He struck the ground like a sack of potatoes, so the two men knew he was dead instantly. They both walked over and looked down at him, then up at Crabbe, who seemed very pleased with himself.

"What was the point of that?" Manning asked.

Crabbe stepped down into the street with them. Men appeared at the batwing doors and windows to look out, but no one stepped outside.

"I thought it might be a good idea to send the Gunsmith a message," Crabbe said.

"And how are we gonna do that?" Manning demanded. "We don't know where he is, unless he's in the saloon and you ain't sayin'."

"Naw, he ain't in there," Crabbe said, "but we don't hafta know where he is."

"And why's that?"

"Because the lawman's horse does," Crabbe said.

Manning and Benson exchanged a glance.

"He might have a point," Benson said. "If we let the horse go and it heads back to wherever Adams is, it *will* send a message."

"You think so, huh?" Manning asked.

Benson shrugged.

"Unless you wanna follow the horse and go up against Adams tonight, in the dark?"

"No," Manning grumbled, "that ain't a good idea."

"Then fine," Crabbe said. "Then let's slap that horse on the rump and get it goin'."

The three men turned the horse so that it was pointed out of town. Benson was about to slap the animal's rump when an idea occurred to Manning and he snapped, "Wait!"

***

Clint heard the horse approaching at a gallop, wondered why Crown was returning so soon, and so quickly. But when he saw the riderless horse, he feared the worst. He was too far outside of town to have heard shots, but he was hoping he was wrong.

As the horse came near, Clint shifted in his saddle so that the Tobiano blocked the animal from going any further. He needn't have bothered. The horse slowed, stopping on its own and just stood there.

Clint dismounted and walked to the animal. There was no indication of violence, no blood or bullet holes on the saddle, but when he walked around to the other side his blood ran cold. There, pinned to Ed Crown's saddlebag, was his badge.

This was a message to Clint Adams, and he got it. Right down to the pit of his stomach, he got it.

Chapter Forty

"Pinnin' the badge to the saddlebag was a good idea," Benson said to Manning.

The two men were seated at a table in Molly's Corner. Crabbe was at the bar, telling some of his men about killing the lawman.

"That's about the only good idea that happened tonight," Manning said.

"Hey, you got to see Crabbe's move," Benson said.

"It wasn't much," Manning said, "considering he was facing a sixty-year-old lawman."

"I told you," Benson said. "He ain't near as fast as he thinks. He goes up against the Gunsmith, he's a dead man."

"Well," Manning said, "maybe we can use him as a diversion."

"You mean," Benson said, "while the Gunsmith's concentratin' on him, we can concentrate on the Gunsmith."

"Right."

"That might work."

"We got a while to think about it," Manning said. "He ain't gonna come in at night."

"What are we gonna do with the dead lawman?"

"I got an idea about that, too," Manning said.

***

By the next morning, the body of Sheriff Ed Crown was on display in a propped up coffin right on Cornville's main street. Clint Adams would not be able to ride in without seeing it.

Manning had the undertaker bring the coffin right to the front of the Golden Ace Saloon, since that was where the lawman had been killed. He, in turn, sat in a chair across the street, in front of the hardware store. He doubted Adams would recognize him on sight, so he felt he was pretty safe sitting out in the open, waiting.

He also had Benson and Crabbe seated on the street, Crabbe right next to the coffin in front of the saloon, and Benson a little further up the street.

Two of Crabbe's men were on rooftops, watching for the Gunsmith so that Manning would get a good warning. The other four men were scattered along the street.

After the shooting the night before, followed by the body being put on display, the people in town knew something was in the wind, so they were staying off the street.

Everybody was just waiting . . .

***

Molly Tanner wasn't waiting.

She knew what was going to happen that day. The dead lawman would surely bring the Gunsmith to town, and he'd be hell-bent-for-vengeance. A man like that would tear through a bunch of two-bit, would–be gunmen.

It was time for her to take her ninety thousand and make her move.

***

Clint found a hill from which he could look down on the town of Cornville. He couldn't see much, just an empty main street. But an empty street told him something. The town was expecting trouble.

It wasn't a large town. He certainly could have circled it and come in from the other direction, but he saw the two men on the rooftops, and they would see him no matter what direction he came from.

But Clint didn't want to sneak into town. They had more than likely killed his friend, and he was going to have to go back to Willow Springs and explain it to Crown's wife, Maggie. When he did that, he wanted to be able to tell her that he had killed the men who killed her husband, and they had seen it coming.

He didn't care how many men were waiting for him in town. He trucked his Colt New Line into his belt, made sure his Peacemaker and rifle were ready for action, and started riding toward town.

***

Molly went to the front of the saloon and looked out the window. She didn't see anybody, but she put down the bag with the money and stepped out the front door to get a better look. She glanced up and down the street, still didn't see anyone. But her saloon was on a corner. She needed to step out further to see down the main street, and that was when she saw Manning seated in front of the hardware store. And she knew he had propped the dead lawman up in front of the Golden Ace Saloon. That meant he was waiting for Clint Adams to come riding in, and he probably had Crabbe and the others with him, which worked for her.

She went back into the empty saloon, picked up the bag of money and headed for the back door.

***

"Rider comin'!" one of Crabbe's men called down from his rooftop.

Manning stood up and stepped into the street.

"Everybody get ready!"

He went back to his chair, because he had decided to give Crabbe his chance, with Benson backing his play, as well as the others. And Manning had something else he needed to do.

He picked up the chair and carried it into the hardware store, then went out the back door.

***

Clint rode slowly down the main street, waiting for someone to take a shot at him. He assumed, with the street as empty as it was, that there were men with guns waiting for him to ride in. The lookouts stationed on the rooftops were also a sign of that.

Everything depended on that first shot missing.

Chapter Forty-One

There was no first shot.

Instead, a man stepped into the street and barred his way. Clint reined the Tobiano in.

"Can I help you?" he asked.

"I'm the man responsible for that," the man said, pointing. Clint looked where he was pointing and saw Ed Crown propped up in a coffin, his shirt front covered with blood.

"So you're the one who sent his horse back to me with his badge pinned to the saddlebag."

"The badge part wasn't my idea, but yeah," the man said. "That was me."

"What's your name?"

"It's Crabbe," the man said, "Buck Crabbe."

"And were you in on the Willow Springs bank job?" Clint asked.

"No," Crabbe said, "I don't do bank robberies. They're too messy."

"But killing a lawman," Clint said, "that's more your style?"

"Actually yeah, it is," Crabbe said. "You're the Gunsmith, right?"

"That's right."

"Then I guess . . . you're next!" Crabbe said, and grabbed for his gun.

Clint had ridden in with his rifle in his left hand, the stock on his thigh, the barrel pointed to the sky. He had the horse's reins in his right hand. He could have dropped them and drawn his pistol, but instead he just let the rifle fall forward and fired it once.

The bullet struck Crabbe in his chest, knocking him over onto his back.

Clint waited for more shots, but none were forthcoming. He dismounted and walked to the fallen man, who was still breathing, although painfully. He looked down at him.

"T-that wasn't fair," Crabbe said. "You didn't even draw your gun."

"Life ain't fair Kid," Clint told him, just before Crabbe died.

He looked up, saw the two men on the rooftops staring down at him, holding rifles. They were apparently waiting for a signal from someone.

"Well, let's go!" Clint shouted. "If we're going to do this, let's do it."

But instead of the volley of shots he was still expecting, another man stepped into the street.

"He was right, you know," the man said. "That wasn't fair. But then he wasn't gonna be a real challenge to you."

"And you will?" Clint asked.

The man, twenty years older than the dead Crabbe, shrugged his shoulders.

"One never knows," he said.

"And what about them?" Clint asked, pointing up. "And I'm sure there are others."

"A few."

"I'm here for the man who held up the bank in Willow Springs and kidnapped a child. And I'm sure he's responsible for that." He pointed at the coffin.

"It was Crabbe who killed the lawman," the man said, "but yeah, the man you want pinned the badge to the saddlebag and put your friend on display."

"And what's that man's name?" Clint asked. "Where is he? Why are you out here fighting his battle?"

"Me? I'm gettin' paid," the man said. "That's all this is to me. A payin' job."

"Is that what it was to him?" Clint asked, pointing to Crabbe?

"Oh no," the man said, "he thought he was gonna make a name for himself by killin' you."

"Too bad it went the other way for him," Clint said. "How about you?

"What about me?"

"You got a name?"

"My name's Benson," the man said, "but you wouldn't know me. I'm nobody. Like I said, just a payin' job."

"I've got an idea," Clint said.

"What's that?"

"Why don't you and your men step down and let whatever his name is deal with his own business?"

"Manning," Benson said. "His name's Manning. I don't think there's any harm in tellin' you that."

No, there wasn't, because Clint already knew the name from talking to Manning's ex-wife in Willow Springs. But he just wanted to make sure.

"And where is Mr. Manning?"

"Oh, he's around here someplace," Benson said, "but I'm afraid I can't step down. See, when I take on a job, I gotta see it through."

"Funny," Clint said, "I'm the same way when I'm doing a favor for a friend."

"Even when the friend is dead?" Benson asked.

Clint looked over at Ed Crown's body, propped up in the coffin, and his stomach went cold.

"Especially when the friend is dead."

Chapter Forty-Two

Des Manning walked to the back door of Molly's Corner and found it not only unlocked, but wide open. He didn't like that. He went inside and made his way to her office. As he entered, he saw that her safe was open. He ran to it, and found that it had some papers in it, but no money.

"Sonofabitch!" he swore.

She'd had the same idea as he did but got to it first. She couldn't have had much of a head start. He ran from the office, out the back door and headed for the livery stable to saddle his horse.

That was when he heard the shots.

***

"So?" Clint asked. "Are we going to do this? You know if we do, you're the first one I'll have to kill. And the only one I really want to kill today is Manning."

"Well, I guess you'll have to go through us first," Benson told him.

"I was afraid you'd say that."

At that point Benson kept his right hand down at his side, by his gun, but brought his left hand up to touch his hat. Even before Clint heard the sound of the guns, he figured this was the signal. Although he knew rifles must be trained on him, seconds from being fired, he still figured he had to deal with Benson, first.

He drew and fired . . .

***

Benson knew it was time to take care of Adams, so he touched his hat, which was the signal. As rifles were trained on the Gunsmith and about to be fired, he saw the man draw and fire. Even before he felt the pain in his chest, he knew he shouldn't have been surprised by the man's speed with his gun, but he was . . . just before he died.

***

After Clint shot Benson, he turned, waved his arms at the Tobiano so the animal would run off, and then dove for cover as bullets began to chew up the street around him.

There were men on the roofs, and both sides of the street, so finding cover wasn't easy. There was a horse trough, but that would only afford him safety from one side of the street. Even as he considered it, bullets from the roof began splashing into the water. He knew he had no choice but to get inside one of the storefronts. That meant breaking down a door or diving through a window.

Deciding quickly, he ran toward a flimsy looking door and ploughed into it with his shoulder. It snapped open and he went stumbling inside, losing his balance, rolling and finally coming to a stop entangled in a collection of dresses.

He was in a woman's store.

He quickly disentangled himself and moved to the window with his rifle ready. The men on the roof were going to have to make an adjustment, so he was only concerned with the men on the ground. They were gathering across the street, putting their heads together, no doubt trying to decide what to do without any of the men who had hired them available to give orders.

He aimed his rifle and fired several shots at the four men, causing them to scatter and duck for cover. He could have killed them, but they weren't high on his kill list, the way Des Manning was.

"You guys look a little confused," Clint called out. "You fellas thinking maybe this isn't your fight?

He watched another couple of men come, both holding rifles. These were the men from the rooftops. They all talked briefly and then there was a lot of nodding.

"You boys have to make up your mind if you want to do this," Clint called out. "I've got to go and find Manning before he leaves town, so make it fast."

He fired one more shot from the rifle, taking one man's hat off with it.

"Come on!" the man bleated.

"If it's all over, walk away," Clint said.

They all put their heads together again, then one asked, "Is that on the level?"

"On the level," Clint said. "Just walk away."

The men looked at each other, then started to drift away one-by-one. But as the last man turned to walk away, Clint shouted again.

"Hold it!"

The man froze.

"Do you know where Manning is?"

"No not for sure," the man said, "but I think I can guess . . ."

Chapter Forty-Three

Clint walked to Molly's Corner, further down the street. The place wasn't open for business, but for some reason the front door was open. Clint took that as a bad sign.

The bartender, Emmett, looked at him in surprise as he entered.

"I'm looking for Des Manning," Clint said.

"I—I don't know, what's goin' on," the bartender said.

"What do you mean?"

"The office in the back," he said, "the boss should be there, but she ain't. And her safe's open. So I don't know what to tell you, Mister. I ain't involved with whatever she and Manning do."

"Back there?"

Emmett pointed.

"That door."

Clint ran to the office and went inside. It was small, and behind a desk was a cannonball safe with the gold paint flaking. He went to it, looked inside, saw only some papers, then hurried back out to the bartender.

"Who's the boss?" Clint asked.

"Her name's Molly Tanner."

"And she and Manning work together?"

"Look, Mister—"

"They killed my friend," Clint said. "He's out there propped up in a coffin. I'm not very happy about that."

"She backs him," the man said. "Bankrolls his jobs and takes a cut. That's all I know."

"Why would the safe be empty, and she's not around?"

"I can only figure she didn't wanna cut him in," the bartender said, "so she lit out. She's always been saying she just needed a big enough stake. I guess she got it."

"That's not going to make Manning happy," Clint said.

"No, sir."

"If he's after her, I have to find them first, before he kills her."

"The livery's at the end of the street," the bartender said. "If she's on the run and he's after her, both their horses'll be gone. Tell Ray I sent ya over."

"Thanks."

"Mr. Adams," Emmett said, "what about the little girl?"

"Do you know where she is?" Clint asked.

"My Mrs. is lookin' after her."

"That's good. I'll have to take her back to her mother in Willow Springs, but if I don't get back . . ."

"Don't worry," Emmett said. "We'll look after her."

"I appreciate that."

"I assume you'll be back for your friend?"

"I will."

"If ya want, I'll get him off the street for ya."

"I'd be much obliged. Now you've got to tell me one more thing."

"What's that?"

"What direction would Molly go?"

"She always said when she had a big enough stake she was goin' to San Francisco. That's all I know."

West.

As Clint went out the door, the bartender knew he had been talking to the Gunsmith. Manning and the others had been waiting for him, and here he was, still walking around after all the shooting. Offering to help him with his dead friend was just the bartender's way of making sure the man had no reason to kill him.

***

Clint reached the livery and saw his Tobiano there. He walked to him and checked him over.

"He yours?" an old hostler asked.

"He is."

"Jus' wandered in here a little while ago," the man said. "I checked him over after I heard the shootin'. He's fine."

"Thanks. Are you Ray?"

"I am."

"The bartender at Molly's sent me over. I'm looking for her horse or Des Manning's horse."

"Well, they're both gone," Ray said. "I figger they rode 'em out."

"Together?"

"I can't tell ya that," Ray said. "I waren't here."

"Can you show me the stall they were in?"

"Sure thing."

Clint followed the man to both stalls, where he examined the hoofprints left by both horses, so he could track them.

"Okay," Clint said. "Thanks."

"Is the shootin' over?" Ray asked, as they walked back to the front of the stable where the Tobiano was waiting.

"It is in town," Clint said. "Here." He gave the man some money. "I'd appreciate it if you'd help the bartender get my dead friend off the street."

"Sure thing, Mr. Adams," Ray said. "We'll get 'im to the undertaker and keep 'im there til you get back."

"And if I don't make it back . . ." Clint said.

"We'll bury 'im for ya."

"I'd appreciate that."

Clint mounted Toby and rode out of the livery. To get out of town, he had to ride back the way he had come. He passed Ed Crown in the propped up coffin, and both Crabbe and Benson, still lying in the street. People were milling about, not sure what to do. They scattered as he rode past.

Chapter Forty-Four

When Manning caught up to Molly, she was sitting on a rock. Standing next to her on three legs was her horse, who was favoring the fourth.

"Trouble?" he asked, riding up to her.

"The stupid animal stepped on something," she said. "Look, Des—"

"Where's the money, Molly?" Manning asked. "In the saddlebags?"

"Now Des—" She stood up, stuck her hands in the back pockets of her jeans. She also had a fur lined vest over her long sleeved shirt.

"Sit back down, Molly," Manning said.

"I didn't mean—"

"Sit!"

Molly sat and Manning walked to her horse. He went through both saddlebags and found them each stuffed with money.

"How much is here?" he asked.

"Des, you don't—"

"How much!"

She firmed her jaw, then said, "Ninety thousand."

"That's a good stake," he said. "Makin' your trip to San Francisco?"

"I thought I—what are you doing?"

He took both saddlebags off her horse.

"You can't take that—only thirty-six-thousand of that is yours. I'll just add my ten per cent to what I already had—"

"That'll just give you fifty-four thousand," Manning said. "That ain't enough for your San Francisco trip." He put the saddlebags on his horse, then turned to face her. "You should just go back to town and start over."

"Start over?" she said, standing again. "You can't take all my money, Des."

"Why not?" he asked. "You were takin' all mine."

"And how am I supposed to get back to town if my horse is lame?"

"Try walkin'," he said. "And walk that horse."

"Will he make it?"

"Just talk to him," Manning said. "Go ahead. Look him in the eye."

Molly walked over to the horse and spoke to Manning while going eye-to-eye with the animal.

"You know, Des, I really wasn't running out on you," she said. "I would have contacted you when I got settled."

"Sure, Molly," he said, coming up behind her. "I know that."

***

Clint saw the lame horse first, then the woman. She was lying on her stomach on the ground. He dismounted and hurried over to her. When he turned her over, she was so limp he knew she was dead. Obviously, Des Manning didn't take it well that she ran out on him with all the money.

He checked the body, found no bullet or stab wounds. He had strangled her to death, probably from behind. He looked at the lame horse again, realized there were no saddlebags.

"I wish I had time to bury you, Molly," he said to the dead woman.

There was a blanket on her horse, so he wrapped the body in it, hoping that would keep critters away until he could return. He also tied the horse to a bush so it wouldn't wander off. Even lame he might be able to use it to transport the body back to Cornville.

Once he had taken care of the body, he checked the ground, saw that Manning was not continuing to move west, but had started south. He mounted up and started following the trail.

Chapter Forty-Five

Clint picked up the hoofprints of Des Manning's horse and fell in behind him. His Tobiano was moving smoothly over the terrain, and he was sure he was going to catch up to Manning before the day was out.

***

Manning hoped the Gunsmith was dead in the Cornville streets and not on his trail, but he pushed his horse, just in case. And that was his mistake. The terrain was hard, and his horse was a big, heavy gelding that was neither light nor surefooted. The same thing happened to it that happened to Molly's mare—the animal took a bad step.

Manning felt it right away. The horse's head dipped as it injured its leg, and Manning reined the animal in and dismounted to check him.

"Sonofabitch," he said, feeling the front left leg. It was already swelling. Hurriedly, he got his canteen, poured some water into his hand and applied it to the swelling, but that wasn't going to do it. He needed a water hole, where the water would be ice cold.

He thought he remembered that there was one up ahead, but he had no idea how long a walk it was going to be. He had no choice but to get started, leading the lame horse.

***

Clint was glad his Tobiano was a surefooted animal.

He could tell by the tracks that Manning's horse had gone lame, and the man was now on foot, leading the animal. Clint hated coincidence, but Molly and Manning's horse's going lame was not a bad one.

"Good boy," he said, patting Toby's neck. "We've just about got him."

***

The sun had hit its zenith and was on the way down when Manning came to the water hole.

"Easy, boy," he said, letting the gelding stand in the ice cold water. "We just have to get the swelling down."

He just needed to be able to ride the animal until he came to a town or a ranch where he could get another one, whether he had to buy it, or steal it.

***

Clint saw the rider and horse standing in the water hole up ahead. Assuming it was Manning, the outlaw and killer was obviously trying to tend to his horse's lameness.

Clint dismounted, tied the Tobiano off to a nearby bush, and started to make his way to the water hole on foot.

***

Manning heard somebody approaching, quickly got himself out of the ankle-deep water, leaving the horse there. He put his hand on his holster and waited. When no one appeared, he got nervous.

"Adams?"

There was some brush around the water hole, and suddenly a man stepped from it.

"I'm going to assume you're Manning," Clint said.

"And that would make you Adams."

"Little problem with your horse?"

"Nothin' I can't handle."

"Maybe it's those heavy saddlebags," Clint said. "I'll just take them off your hands."

Manning laughed.

"That's rich."

"No," Clint said, "you think you're rich, but you're not. I don't know how much money you killed three people in Willow Springs, a school teacher and now Molly Tanner for. Five people? Are there more I don't know about?"

"How many have you killed?"

"You mean today?" Clint asked. "Just the ones you left behind to fight your battles. That is, the ones who weren't smart enough to walk away."

"You musta scared about half a dozen of them off, then," Manning said.

"Yeah," Clint said, "Benson and a fellow named Crabbe weren't that smart."

"You know," Manning said, "it was Crabbe who killed your friend, the sheriff."

"That's true," Clint said, "but you pinned his badge to his horse and propped him up in a coffin."

Manning licked his lips.

"Look, Adams," he said, "there's ninety thousand in those saddlebags. Why don't you take half?"

"Because I'm not a money hungry killer," Clint said. "That's all you."

"Goddamn you, man!" Manning said, and went for his gun, knowing full well he wasn't going to make it.

Clint drew and fired. Manning staggered back several steps, fell onto his back in the water in front of his horse.

"No," Clint said, "God is going to damn you."

Coming January 27, 2021

THE GUNSMITH
466
Young Butch Cassidy

For more information
visit: www.SpeakingVolumes.us

On Sale Now!
THE GUNSMITH GIANT
No. 1
Trouble in Tombstone

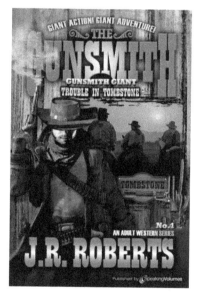

**For more information
visit:** www.SpeakingVolumes.us

On Sale Now!

THE GUNSMITH *series*
Books 430 - 464

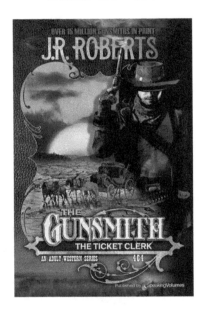

For more information
visit: www.SpeakingVolumes.us

On Sale Now!

TALBOT ROPER NOVELS
by
ROBERT J. RANDISI

For more information
visit: www.SpeakingVolumes.us

On Sale Now!

Lady Gunsmith *series*
Books 1 - 9
Roxy Doyle and the Lady Executioner

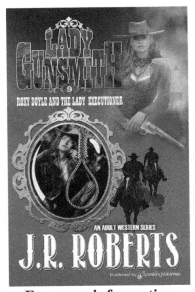

For more information
visit: www.SpeakingVolumes.us

On Sale Now!

Award-Winning Author
Robert J. Randisi (J.R. Roberts)

For more information
visit: www.SpeakingVolumes.us

Sign up for free and bargain books

Join the Speaking Volumes mailing list

Text

ILOVEBOOKS

to 22828 to get started.

Message and data rates may apply.

CPSIA information can be obtained
at www.ICGtesting.com
Printed in the USA
LVHW031729180521
687788LV00005B/263

9 781645 403609